THE PRAIRIE FIRE WITHIN

By C.D. Melley

THE PRAIRIE FIRE WITHIN

Copyright © Douglas J. McLeod, 2014

Melley, C.D. 1971 –

The Prairie Fire Within

Second Edition

ISBN-13: 978-0991713783

ISBN: 0991713788

1.   Romance – Fiction. 2. Saskatchewan – Fiction.

This book is set in Times New Roman

Acknowledgements

This book would not have come to pass without the support of some wonderful people along the way.

First, to my darling wife-to-be, Catherine; we've been through a lot together during our time together, but for however rough our journey has been, I consider it a blessing every day that we've found each other. I love you with all my heart.

I would be remised not to mention the woman who inspired me in all of my writing endeavours, my late Great Aunt Pat. There's not a day that goes by where I'm not thinking about her. She was a great woman, and I hope my writing will provide a legacy in her memory that will last forever.

Finally, I would like to recognize all of the people who have helped me during this literary journey: Bethlyn, Jen F., Danielle, Cassandra, Christa, Jen H., and Jen A. You gals gave me the encouragement to dive into this world of romance writing, and I thank you all for guiding me along the way.

CHAPTER ONE

"Aunt Evelyn, can I go play in the fields?"

"Of course you may, Amanda dear. You can call your Uncle Gerald in; it's almost time for lunch."

A 10-year old Amanda Bellamy ran out of the farm house, and into the field of towering corn stalks behind the dwelling. She always enjoyed spending her summers on the farm outside of Melville, Saskatchewan. It enabled her to get away from the daily trudges of grade school in Regina. Like most children, Amanda despised having to learn "the three R's." However, when school let out every June, she eagerly counted down the days until she could head to her Uncle Gerald and Aunt Evelyn's farm.

Life was simple on the Prairies. If you grew up on the farm, you worked on it. While wheat is the renowned crop grown in the province, Melville possessed some of the most fertile land for corn production in the region. While Amanda was a mere child, she did her fair share to help out when she could; sweeping up the barn while her uncle was working out in the fields, or helping her aunt in the kitchen to make sure everyone was fed after a hard day toiling in the prairie sun. Whenever she wasn't pulling her own weight, Amanda spent her days playing with her cousins, Rebecca and Leonard. Most children in the big city would rather be playing outside; trying to get as much fun from their time off at the park or swimming pool. Not for Amanda; she loved being with her aunt and uncle, regardless of her capacity.

Amanda ran towards the combine being piloted by her uncle Gerald. "Uncle Gerald! Uncle Gerald!" she called out to him. The

1

elder relative continued to harvest his crop until he saw his young niece approach the machine. He stopped his vehicle momentarily so he could hear what the young girl had to say. Gerald Brimley was a balding gentleman, but hid his barren scalp with green baseball cap. His build was stocky, but his heart was just as big. He loved Amanda like she was one of his own children.

"Uncle Gerald," she panted, "Aunt Evelyn said it's time to come in for lunch."

"Thanks for letting me know, Amanda. Here, climb on in. We'll drive back to the house together."

Gerald helped his niece into the cabin of his combine. As the two drove back to the barn, Amanda wrapped her little arms around her uncle's burly arm, and smiled; happy to be with her adoring relative.

~ * * * ~

It was a rainy spring day in Toronto, and Amanda was swamped with work; mountains of file folders were piled upon her desk. She was a 30-year old advertising executive for a big corporation. It had been five years since she graduated with her MBA from the University of Saskatchewan, and she had settled into her role as someone who lived and worked in the big city. However, there were moments during her hectic schedule where she pined for the simpler days of her youth. She yearned to return to the prairie haven for some well-deserved R & R, but with the stack of files growing, any opportunity to get away for a week appeared to be dwindling with no sign of returning anytime soon.

Amanda was toiling away on her latest project when her secretary buzzed her.

"Your cousin Leonard is on Line 2, Miss Bellamy," the secretary reported.

"Thank you, Stephanie," Amanda said before picking up the phone. "Leonard, it's so good to hear your voice."

"Hello, Amanda," he said. "I hope I'm not disturbing you at work."

"No," she said. "I'm working on an account here."

Leonard picked up on the stress in his cousin's voice, "It sounds like you need a break there."

Amanda winced in mental agony. "You don't know the half of it," she replied. "I've got files coming out of my ears here. I need to get away from it all for a few days, but I don't think I will be able to anytime soon."

Leonard's voice became solemn. "Well," he said, "I think I might have a 'get out of work free' card for you."

Amanda joked, "Did you win the lottery, and are offering to take the whole family to Florida for a vacation?"

Leonard sighed. "I wish that were the case," he said, "but I'm afraid I'm the bearer of bad news."

Amanda grew concerned. "What's wrong?" she asked. "Are things alright with your wife?"

The pain was evident in Leonard's voice. "Things with Linda are good," he reported, "but it's my dad, Amanda. He passed away a couple of days ago."

3

Amanda didn't say a word at first, but a couple of tears began to trickle down her cheek. Her voice cracked when she spoke, "Uncle Gerald's gone? I'm so sorry, Leonard. Have they determined what the cause of death was?"

"The doctor said it was from old age," Leonard said. "Dad asked about you in his dying days, but he knew you were busy with your job."

Leonard's words cut through Amanda's heart like a knife. Even on his death bed, he still talked about her. Had she known Gerald was at death's door, she would've dropped everything and flown out to Saskatchewan to spend some of his last moments with him. Alas, it was too late to do so now.

"Damn this job," Amanda swore. "I wish I could have been by his bedside."

"Considering how busy you are there," Leonard said, "I'm not sure you would've gotten clearance to come out here."

"That's hard to say," she said. "Uncle Gerald isn't immediate family, but this is me wondering after the fact. Have you decided when the funeral will be?"

"It's scheduled for this Saturday in Melville," he reported.

"I'll be there," she pronounced. "It's the least I could do."

"That would be wonderful, Amanda," Leonard said, "but what about your work?"

Amanda sighed. "At this point," she said, "my job is insignificant. I missed Uncle Gerald's last days; I'll be damned if I don't go to the funeral to say goodbye to him."

Leonard replied, "I'll let Linda know you'll be coming out, and we'll get the guest room ready."

"You don't have to do that," Amanda said. "I can stay in a hotel."

"Nonsense," he said. "You are part of my family. You're staying with us, I insist."

"Thank you, Leonard," Amanda said. "I'll let my supervisors know I'll be leaving Friday for a few days. They won't like it, but they should understand since it *is* family. I'll email you my itinerary once I have my flight booked."

"Alright then," he said. "I'll see you sometime Friday."

Amanda hung up her phone and buried her face in her hands; fighting back the tears. All of the memories of the times she shared with Gerald are all she had left of him. However, she thought of her cousins. If the news of Gerald's passing was hitting her hard, Leonard and Rebecca must have been shattered. They lost their mother three years before due to old age, now their dad was gone. While the Brimley children were all grown-up now, not having Gerald and Evelyn around to see their grandchildren grow up was disheartening. Rebecca had no children of her own that Amanda knew of, but she knew Leonard and Linda had a son of their own; little Nathan, born five years ago. He was at an age where he was still too young to comprehend the fact his grandfather wasn't going to be around anymore, but would grow to miss him in his later years.

Amanda composed herself, walked to her supervisor's office, and let him know of the tragic news. Mr. Lawrence was understanding of the situation, and told his junior executive to take a few days off to grieve; a relief to the stressed-out Amanda. Afterwards, she returned to her office, told Stephanie to hold all her calls, and cried some more before checking the internet for the first available flight to Regina.

CHAPTER TWO

The service was a solemn one, as everyone from the Brimley family tree attended. The Saskatchewan skies were gray, and a light rain fell from the heavens when they laid Gerald to rest. The ensuing wake was filled with fond memories of the kind-hearted man who toiled in the corn fields. However, Rebecca was causing a stink; worried about what was to become of the property. An argument she continued at the reading of Gerald's will a couple of days later.

She, along with Amanda, Leonard, and his wife, Linda gathered in the office of Gerald's lawyer, Robert Mitchell to learn what would become of their departed relative's holdings. Amanda choked back her tears, and Leonard sought comfort with his wife, but Rebecca had become melodramatic.

She complained, "I hate having to deal with all of this."

Leonard said, "I'm not a fan of it either, but Dad lived a full life. You have to commend him for remaining strong after Mum passed away."

"It's still sad that he's no longer with us," Amanda said. "I can still picture him in his tractor; tilling the fields, so he could prepare them for planting the year's corn crop."

Linda said, "He didn't have to do that in recent years, did he?"

"No," Leonard explained. "He hired a small staff of farm hands to help him out. Two hundred acres is a fair amount of agricultural land to maintain with the workers he has; let alone doing it all by himself."

7

Amanda said, "It's still formidable he was able to make a living out of it for as long as he did."

"Far too long, if you ask me," Rebecca commented. "I wanted him to sell the farm after Mum passed on, and retire to the city. But, Dad was set in his ways; he didn't want to part with the so-called 'family business.'"

Leonard said, "You can't blame him for that. After Mum died, it was all he had left."

"Yes," Rebecca huffed, "and look where he is now: a lonely man who's now six feet underground."

The other three were shocked by Rebecca's bitter words. They understood she was upset over Gerald's passing, but for her to spew such venomous hatred wasn't going to bring him back. Even if he did sell the farm, what purpose would it have served? Would he have been able to socialize with others in the city? Or, would he have been ostracized by them because he was an outsider? But, excluding others was not the Saskatchewan way.

The province had a rich sense of community, regardless if you lived in booming metropolises like Regina and Saskatoon, or if you hailed from a smaller town like Melville or Rouleau. It was the feeling of a regional family showcased ten times a year where people from all corners of Saskatchewan would congregate on Piffles Taylor Way to celebrate the province's unofficial religion; with its parishioners clad in their finest green and white. Farming was a livelihood here, and to turn their backs on someone who chose it as their way of living was not in line with the common line of thinking. It was akin to someone who favoured the bright lights of the big metropolises in other parts of the country; the same cities where Amanda had returned home from for the reason of Gerald's passing. However, they wondered why Rebecca was reacting this way. Why did she want her father to turn her back on the only life he had ever known, and to "get with the modern times?" None of the others knew of her true motives, but it was a mindset they believed sullied the good name of Gerald Brimley. But, before the scene turned into a verbal altercation, Robert Mitchell entered the office.

The lawyer said, "I'm sorry for my tardiness, everyone. I was in court with another client."

Leonard said, "No apologies are necessary, Mr. Mitchell. We appreciate the time you're giving us."

Linda added, "Although, we wish it were under better circumstances."

"Yes," Mr. Mitchell said. "I'm sorry for your loss. Mr. Brimley was a good man; however, I'm sure he's in a better place now."

Rebecca sighed and said, "I don't want to sound morbid, but at least he'll be happy now that he's been reunited with Mum."

Leonard stared daggers at his sister. Rebecca had a lot of gall to make such a comment after what she said earlier, but she was right. Gerald could live in peace since he and Evelyn were together once again.

Mr. Mitchell said, "If everyone is ready I will now read the Last Will and Testament of Mr. Gerald Brimley."

The four members of Gerald's family let out a collective sigh of despair for their loss, but sat attentively during the reading. Amanda glanced over at Rebecca, and noticed the cousin was putting on a show of crocodile tears. Yes, Rebecca was upset over her father's passing; however, with her earlier comments regarding her wishes, Amanda knew it was all a façade.

The executor continued...

> *I, Gerald Brimley, being of sound mind and body,*
> *do hereby bequeath the following: To my loving*
> *son Leonard and his wife, Linda...*

Leonard took a deep breath, and braced himself for the declaration.
He took Linda's hand into his for moral support.

> *The two of you found each other fifteen years ago,*
> *and were able to showcase the same amount of*
> *love I shared with my dearly beloved Evelyn. You*
> *both brought me great joy when you brought my*
> *sweet grandson, Nathan, into the world ten years*
> *later. I am eternally grateful for this gift, and for*
> *that, I bequeath all of my investments, so you may*
> *establish an education fund for him to attend*
> *whatever college or university he desires once he*
> *graduates from high school.*

Linda cried tears of joy as her husband held her in a loving
embrace. She said, "What a gracious reward. Now, we can afford
to send little Nate to the University of Saskatchewan."

Leonard said, "Depending on what's in those investments, we
could send him to law school at McGill, if his heart desires."

With her brother and his wife obtaining Gerald's nest egg, Rebecca
rubbed her hands in anticipation of what she might receive in the
Will. She hoped it would be his farm, so she could sell it to the
highest bidder, and reap all of the proceeds from it. When Leonard
and Linda saw how Rebecca was behaving, they both said a silent
prayer in hopes their sister would not get her hands on the prized
family business.

> *To my darling niece, Amanda:*

I like to think of you as one of my own children.
You have been successful in everything you have
done. However, I must confess, I have been
dismayed over your life in the fast-paced
advertising industry; how it has robbed your
ability to slow down and enjoy the simple things
life has to offer. I know you never had the
opportunity to stop and smell the proverbial roses
since you went off to university; therefore, I am
bequeathing you my corn farm outside of Melville.
This way, you can escape to the country anytime
your heart desires.

Amanda didn't say a word, but she felt the jealous, cold stare from
Rebecca. Gerald's daughter was seething over the fact he had
given the family business to someone who wasn't part of the
immediate family. Rebecca felt it should have gone to her, not
some outsider. Regardless, it was news that brought relief to both
Leonard and Linda.

Finally, to my daughter, Rebecca:

You are my first born, and you should be given the
best I have to offer. However, as you grew older, it
became clear to me you were adamant about
wanting me to leave the industry that has provided
for both yourself and your brother in favour of the
sedentary life. What you have failed to understand
is we are a family steeped in the agricultural
industry. What we do is provide the tools to feed
not only ourselves, but others around the world.
Agriculture is the lifeblood of any culture; for our
health and well-being. You have chosen to ignore

this premise, and because of such, you will not be receiving anything from my estate.

Amanda watched as Rebecca became livid over the announcement. "How dare Dad," Rebecca yelled. "I'm the one who's been part of his life the longest outside of Mum. I'm the one who should be getting the investments, or the farm. This is an outrage!"

Before Leonard could open his mouth, his sister threatened to contest the Will in court. A furious Rebecca stormed out of Mr. Mitchell's office, and slammed the door behind her in a huff. The rest of the family in attendance were upset over Rebecca's outburst. The executor provided a voice of reason.

He said, "I can understand she's upset over the revelations, but Miss Brimley doesn't have a leg to stand on."

Amanda asked, "Are you sure about that, Mr. Mitchell? Rebecca was adamant about taking the document to trial."

"I assure you, Miss Bellamy," Mr. Mitchell replied, "it is ironclad. I've been a lawyer for twenty-five years, and unless your cousin can provide medical documentation proving your uncle Gerald was not in the right mental capacity when he wrote his Will, what was written in here is final."

Leonard said, "Trust me, Amanda, Linda and I were around Dad as much as Rebecca was, and he showed no sign of Alzheimer's or any other mental incapacity. Should she try to take this to court, I will testify in Dad's favour."

"Thank you, Leonard," Amanda said, "but this is so surreal to me. I own Uncle Gerald's farm? I'm flattered and honoured to be in possession of it, but I have no idea how to run a farm. I don't know where to begin."

Linda said, "Don't worry, hon. When Gerald fell ill, the farm hands managed the day-to-day operations; making sure the crops were harvested, and the fields prepared for the next growing season."

Leonard said, "Plus, if you need a hand with anything, you have my number. Linda and I will be there to help you get reacquainted with how the farm is run."

Amanda sat there while the whole notion sank in. A woman, who left the province where she grew up to become an advertising executive in the biggest city in the country, was given the title to a humble blue-collar operation. She hadn't been on a farm in years, but Amanda Bellamy was about to be reunited with the simple life of her youth.

CHAPTER THREE

The day after the reading of Gerald's Will, Leonard drove Amanda to the place where she spent her childhood summers: Gerald's farm on the outskirts of Melville. When she arrived, she noticed not much had changed over the years. The family homestead was still the modest two-story farmhouse, but there was the addition of an adjoining guest house 200 yards away built for the staff Gerald had hired on to reside. The chickens Amanda tended to as a child had been sold off, but the barn where she cared for them was still standing; a new coat of paint had been applied to the structure since she was last on the property five years prior.

Leonard asked, "So, what do you think of the old place?"

Amanda said, "Aside from a few cosmetic changes, it looks the same as it did when I was last out here for Nathan's birth."

"Oh, right," he remembered. "You weren't able to make it out for Mum's funeral."

"Believe me, I wanted to come out for it," she said, "but I was just settling into my new job in Toronto, and I couldn't get the time off. I'm surprised Mr. Lawrence gave me the opportunity to come out this time around."

Leonard reasoned, "I guess he realized how disheartened you were when Mum passed on three years ago, and didn't want you to deny the same opportunity to say goodbye to Dad."

Amanda shrugged. "Perhaps," she said, "but maybe he sensed I was overworked at the office lately, and thought some time off would do me some good."

"You're going to have a huge stack of files when you get back, aren't you?" he asked.

"Most likely," she said, "but as you know, I brought my laptop with me, so I've been able to work on some of the accounts while I haven't been grieving."

Leonard laughed. "I'll know who to send my internet bill to, then," he said. "My bandwidth charges will be through the roof for this weekend alone."

Amanda smacked her cousin's arm. "I'll just deduct it as a business expense," she said. "Mr. Lawrence should be good about it, given my circumstance."

"But, what if he isn't?" Leonard asked.

"Then, that's something I'll have to take up with him when I get back to the office," Amanda said, "whenever that may be."

Leonard helped Amanda with her bags to the upstairs bedroom. She thought it would be a good idea to stay at the farm for a couple of weeks, so she could familiarize herself with the property and the operations. Since she was the new owner and proprietor, Amanda wanted to try and help out wherever she could, and get acquainted with the people she will be managing. Gerald didn't employ a huge staff; four people resided in the guest house, but if they were going to keep things afloat they needed to work together as a cohesive unit.

"I guess I should introduce myself to the others," Amanda said.

"It couldn't hurt," Leonard replied. "Come on, I'll bring you to them."

Leonard led Amanda to the barn, so she could meet the staff. Three of the farmhands were out in the fields, and were making their way back to the homestead when they saw Leonard's car in the driveway. When they entered the barn, they were met by a woman who recognized Gerald's son right away.

"Morning, Leonard," the woman said.

"Morning, Ashley," Leonard greeted. "How are things going?"

"It's been difficult with your dad's passing," Ashley said, "but we're making due the best that we can; my condolences, by the way."

"Thank you," he said. "I'd like to introduce you to my cousin. Amanda Bellamy, meet Ashley Washburn. She's one of the people who help out around here."

Amanda extended her hand to Ashley. "Pleased to meet you," she said.

Ashley shook Amanda's hand. "Likewise," she said. "So, you're the one who left Saskatchewan to become the advertising executive in Toronto. Gerald told us about you. He was disappointed when you left for the big city, but he always spoke fondly of you."

"Well, you'll be seeing me more often," Amanda announced. "I inherited the farm."

"That's wonderful," Ashley said. "I hope you can use some of your marketing expertise to help negotiate a better stipend from the government for us farmers."

Leonard said, "I'm not sure Amanda is trained to deal with the bureaucrats in Ottawa."

Ashley blew him off. "Nonsense," Ashley stated. "A pretty face like hers is sure to swing a few fat cats into our favour."

Amanda blushed. "Thank you for the compliment," she said, "but I figured since I own the place, I should get reacquainted with the operations, and make sure the place is running smoothly."

A voice called out from outside of the barn. "Hey Ashley, is Leonard in the barn with you?"

Another voice added, "We saw his car in the driveway, but didn't see him in the main house."

"He's in here, guys," Ashley yelled out, "and he brought our new boss with him!"

Loud muttering was heard amongst those in the barn.

"I'm not sure I can handle new blood," the first voice spoke.

"I hope they're not a complete hard ass. Gerald was pretty easy-going with us," the second person said.

"Quiet, you two," a third voice with an Alberta accent stated. "They can probably hear you. You haven't met the new boss yet, and already you're making a bad impression."

The three men entered the barn, and made their way to the others.

"Boys," Ashley introduced, "I'd like you to meet Gerald's cousin, Amanda. She got the farm in his Will, and came by to see how things work around here."

Amanda was nervous after hearing their comments outside. She waved to them, and said, "Hi, guys."

The three men individually stepped forward, and formally shook their new supervisor's hand. The first was a lanky male with short black hair, covered by a black baseball cap. "Kevin Matthews," he introduced himself. The second was wearing a pair of overalls and sported stringy brown hair. "Cecil Hicks," he stated. However, it was the third male who would make Amanda speechless. He stood six-foot-two, and short blond hair with a bit of a spike, and ice-blue eyes. He wore blue jeans and a buttoned-down plaid shirt. "Hello, Amanda," he said. "I'm Hank Acker."

Amanda stood there in silence, as she heard Hank's voice. He was the one with the western twang she heard, telling Kevin and Cecil to behave. Hank sounded like he should have been recording songs in Nashville, instead of working in the corn fields outside of Melville, Saskatchewan. It was a voice that was quite attractive to Amanda, and if it wasn't for the others standing in the barn with her, she might have been bold to ask Hank out based on the accent alone. Amanda always had initiative; it was what prompted her to move to Toronto after graduating to improve her employment chances. However, recognizing her surroundings, Amanda remained calm and professional.

"It's a pleasure to meet you all," she said, "and I look forward to working with you."

Ashley said, "Amanda works as an advertising executive in Toronto, so she's going to be trained on how things work around here."

The male members of the crew grew more hesitant. "You've never worked on a farm before?" Cecil asked.

Amanda explained, "I helped out with Uncle Gerald and Aunt Evelyn when I was younger, but I haven't been back here since I graduated from U of S."

"So, you're a Husky?" Kevin said. "Welcome home."

"Thanks, Kevin," Amanda said. "I'm only here for a couple of weeks so I can get a lay of the land. I want to be able to carry on the 'family business' like Gerald wanted me to."

Cecil muttered, "That might be difficult from a corner office on Bay Street. We need someone who can be here on a daily basis." Ashley nudged Cecil in the ribs in a bid to get him to behave.

Sensing the bubbling tension, Leonard checked his watch. "It's almost lunchtime," he said. "Why don't we rustle up some food, and we can discuss things more at length."

Ashley agreed. "Good idea," she said. "We can grab a bite to eat, and Amanda can tell us more about herself."

The group of six headed into the homestead and whipped together some quick sandwiches. Amanda regaled her support staff with her memories of spending her summers on the farm as a child, and in turn, the others filled her in on how the crops are planted, harvested, and processed. The guys on the staff were still reluctant to welcome the new owner into the fold. However, they put on a welcoming facade to her.

The six shared their memories of Gerald, and Amanda informed them of how much of a wonderful woman Evelyn was. The chat softened Kevin's hesitation, and Cecil began to come around. However, Hank was the toughest nut to crack. He remained a consummate professional at the dining room table; yet, whenever he recalled his time spent with her uncle, Amanda was daydreaming. She was becoming lost in the sound of the blond-haired man's voice; his drawl was so appealing. Amanda would've drifted away from reality had it not been for Kevin's question.

He asked, "So Amanda, are you involved with anyone back in Toronto?"

Ashley scolded him. "Kevin, that's not the type of question you should be asking your boss. What goes on in her private life is none of our business."

Amanda broke from her trance. "Alas, my job is the only thing I'm married to," she said. "I don't get much of an opportunity to let my hair down because I'm always working on a project."

Ashley said, "Well then, before you head back, we should take you out for a night on the town. Mind you, we don't have any of the fancy clubs they have in Toronto, but the five of us can go out, have a few drinks, and toast the memory of Gerald Brimley together."

"I'm up for that," Cecil said.

"Me too," Kevin added.

"What about you, Hank?" Ashley asked. "Are you in?"

Hank thought about it for a second. He didn't want to be the odd one out for the planned soiree. However, he considered the purpose of the proposed outing. After a moment, he gave his answer. "What the hell," he said, "for Gerald."

Everyone agreed, "For Gerald."

Amanda asked, "Would you like to join us, Leonard?"

He said, "I don't know if Linda will let me out. I'm not allowed to party like I used to since Nathan was born."

"I'll talk to her if you want me to," Ashley said. "Hell, I might even convince her to leave Nate at the sitter, and you can both come."

"Let me run it by her first," Leonard said, "and we can go from there."

"That sounds fair enough," Ashley said. "Personally, I think it would be better if all seven of us got together to honour him. We were the closest to him."

Amanda asked, "Should we extend an invite to Rebecca?"

Everyone glared at the Torontonian, as if she cursed the whole group. Amanda worried about losing the goodwill she had just built with everyone at the table. Things were rocky when she was introduced to the staff by Leonard. Did she throw it all away with that one question?

Ashley said, "With all due respect, Amanda, after we heard how she reacted at the reading of the Will, Rebecca is persona non grata."

Cecil said, "If she got her hands on this place, she'd sell it off, and all of us would lose our jobs and the nice little spread we have in the guest house. We can't let her do that to us, nor Gerald and Evelyn's legacy."

Amanda chose her next words carefully. "Alright then," she said, "just the five or seven of us. I could use a night out."

Leonard said, "We all could, Amanda. The past few days have been stressful for all of us, and we need a chance to unwind."

Hank said, "Then, it's settled: next Friday night, we're going to hit the bar in town and honour Gerald."

The group of six finished their lunch, and returned back to their duties. Kevin, Cecil, and Hank went back out into the fields, and Ashley headed towards the barn. Leonard made sure Amanda was settled in her temporary room before giving her a hug; telling her, "Call me if you need someone to talk to." After he drove away, Amanda flopped onto her bed; revelled in the feel of the soft linens, and caught a quick nap. However, as she slept, the only thing she could think about was Hank and his voice.

She thought to herself, "I'm going to have to pick Ashley's brain about him. He's not much on the exterior, but that hair, those eyes, and that voice? I wonder if he might be interested in a girl like me; provided I didn't stick my foot too far into my mouth during lunch."

Amanda spent the next couple of hours trying to think of how to approach her female counterpart on the subject.

CHAPTER FOUR

The next day, as the midday shone down on the prairie, everyone was working hard around the farm. The boys were busy tilling the fields and planting the season's corn crop, while Ashley continued to putter around the barn. Amanda saved the file she was toiling away with on her laptop, and decided to get to work on preparing a hearty meal for her crew. She made her way to the kitchen and checked the pantry to see what she could whip up. After some scrounging, she settled on making a huge pot of spaghetti and meatballs. It seemed simplistic, but it was the quickest and easiest thing to cook. For an added touch, she found a frozen garlic loaf in the freezer, and threw it into the oven for a tantalizing side; along with preparing a fresh salad to go along with the meal.

It was 5:30 when everything was ready. By the time Amanda rang the dinner bell, her crew were famished. They made their way to the dining room and devoured the meal as if it were the last one they would receive before being executed on Death Row. The whole time, Amanda could not take her eyes off of Hank. There was something about him that made him appealing to her eyes, but she wondered if there was something more to him than what she had seen so far. Amanda wasn't the type of woman who was into scruffy faces, sparkling eyes, or a certain accent; all of which Hank possessed. She liked her men buff; muscular and well-groomed. However, there was still something that allured her to Hank. The only problem was, because of his attire, Amanda couldn't tell if Hank was a certifiable hunk.

Ashley waved her hand in front of Amanda's face, and asked, "Earth to Amanda, this is Ground Control. Do you copy?"

The heir snapped to her senses. "I'm sorry," she apologized. "What's going on?"

Hank repeated, "I said, 'I figured we'll be finished planting this year's crop in another few days.'"

Amanda hung on his every word. "That's excellent news," she said.

Kevin quipped, "If I didn't know any better, I'd say our new boss is smitten with Hank."

Amanda denied the accusation. "I am not," she replied. "It's unprofessional for me to do such a thing. It's just... I find accents in general to be an attractive trait."

Hank chuckled. "I didn't realize I had one," he said.

Ashley interrupted. "I hate to be the one to clue you in, Hank," she said, "but you do. There is a certain Albertan twang to it."

Attempting to steer the conversation away from her apparent attraction, Amanda asked the group, "So, everyone knows about my back story. What about the rest of you? Where are all of you from, and how did you come into working with my uncle?"

Cecil began the responses. "It's a funny story," he said. "But, I met Gerald at a Riders' game. I was fortunate enough to score a ticket to the Labour Day Classic three years ago, and Gerald happened to be sitting beside me. We got to talking, and he told me there was an opening here at the farm to come help him out. I had just graduated from the University of Regina the previous April, and was having a hard time looking for work. Gerald came through for me, and I've been with him ever since."

Kevin spoke next. "I actually worked with Gerald as part of a placement while I was studying at Parkland College in Yorkton," he explained. He liked my work ethic so much he offered me a full-time position when I finished my program. I've been thankful for the opportunity."

Ashley replied, "To be honest, I went outside of the province to earn my agricultural degree; getting my education at the University of Guelph in Ontario. When I graduated, I came back to Melville and ran into Kevin. He told me about how much of a great guy Gerald was, and suggested I ask him if he had any openings. So, I swung by the farm, had an interview with him, and he hired me on the spot. He said I reminded him a bit of you, but in reverse order."

Amanda turned her attention to the man who she had been daydreaming about the previous couple of days. "What about you, Hank?" she asked. "How did you find your way out here to Melville?"

Hank looked straight into Amanda's jade eyes and said, "I have to confess, I've been a journeyman. I've travelled all around the Prairies, doing the odd job here or there. That was until I rolled into town, and asked around for a job. Gerald was the one man who was willing to give me a break. He appreciated the hard work I was willing to put in around here, and offered me a full-time position. By that time, Cecil was already here, and a few weeks later, Kevin came into the fold; followed by Ashley. I never had much of a family growing up, but with everybody here, I felt like I finally had one. It's a shame I never had the opportunity to meet Evelyn. I'm sure she would've made a great 'den mother' to us all."

Amanda's heart skipped a beat after hearing Hank's story. If it wasn't for the others, she would've walked over to him and given him a huge hug. The only problem was, if she did, she might not have let him go; plus, it would make her look bad in front of everyone. She regained her composure and replied, "Aunt Evelyn was a wonderful woman. She shared the same warmth and compassion Gerald had. You would have loved and admired her; as much as, you did for Uncle Gerald. I'm sure both of them are thankful all of you have remained after their passing to help keep this place afloat."

Everyone at the table looked down at the table, downtrodden.

"The farm is doing alright, isn't it?" Amanda asked.

Ashley looked up at her supervisor. "If truth be told," she said, "things have been kind of tight around here."

Amanda blinked. "What do you mean?" she asked. "I thought this place was doing quite well."

Kevin replied, "To be honest, it hasn't. As you know, Gerald didn't leave anything for us in his Will, and most of our savings have dried up trying to keep this place running when he fell ill."

"It's a surprise we're able to even plant this year's crop," Cecil added. "The weather last year hurt us severely."

"Didn't Uncle Gerald receive any insurance money to help cover the losses?" Amanda asked.

Cecil replied, "He received some, but it was barely enough to scrape by."

"That's why I asked if you could help us with the province," Ashley said. "Without any subsidies, if the bad weather returns, the farm will be bankrupt."

26

Amanda sat in silence as the news sank in with her. No wonder Rebecca wanted to sell the farm if she got her hands on it. If Gerald's business was doing this poorly, Rebecca would be able to turn some profit on it from its sale. The only downside to the scenario would be the loss of the jobs and home for the staff. There was no guarantee the new owners would hire them on, or if the farm would continue to produce food. For all anyone at the table knew, the plot of land could be sold to a developer who would turn the family business into a housing development for families immigrating to Saskatchewan.

Amanda sighed. "I'll see what I can do," she said. "I'll be damned if this is the way Uncle Gerald's legacy ends. This farm has been his lifeblood, and has provided means for all of you. I don't know if I'll be successful in appealing to the government, but for Uncle Gerald, it's the least I can do."

Any previous ill will the staff felt towards Amanda began to melt away. The notion of their new boss going to bat for the farm, and for them, cast Gerald Brimley's niece in a different light. They didn't know if she would be able to jump through the necessary hoops, given her hectic job back in Toronto, but with Amanda in their corner doing some additional legwork, at least they had a fighting chance.

Amanda reached for the serving dish. "Does anybody want any more spaghetti?" she asked.

"No thanks," Ashley replied. "I'm stuffed."

"Me too," Cecil added.

"I couldn't eat another bite," Kevin stated.

"Well then," Amanda declared, "I guess I'll start clearing the table."

Hank stood up and said, "Please, Amanda. You made a wonderful dinner for us. The least we can do is to do that and wash the dishes for you."

"Are you sure about that?" she asked. "You guys have been out in the fields all day."

Kevin gathered a couple of plates. "We insist," he answered.

Amanda smiled. "Thank you, guys," she said. "It's greatly appreciated."

Ashley announced, "I'll clean the pots."

"Actually, Ashley," Amanda interrupted, "could I have a word with you in private, please?"

Cecil quipped, "Uh oh, Ashley's in the dog house already."

"It's not that," the heir clarified. "I just want to have a girl talk with her."

Kevin nudged Hank in the ribs, almost upsetting the glasses he was gathering. "I wonder what *those* two are going to be talking about."

Hank barked, "Damn it, Kevin, watch what you're doing! You almost made me smash them on the floor."

~ * * * ~

The women retreated to Amanda's room, and the supervisor shut the door behind them.

"I don't want the guys to hear us," she explained.

"I'm going to guess you want us to dish about one of them," Ashley presumed.

"Yes," Amanda confirmed, "specifically Hank."

Ashley rolled her eyes. "I should have known you wanted to talk to me about him," she said.

"So, what's his deal?" Amanda asked. "Is he seeing somebody? Tell me all that you know about him."

"Easy there, Amanda," Ashley cautioned. "You may have googly eyes for Hank, but you just met him yesterday. Don't you think your hormones are raging a little too hard?"

Amanda resigned herself. "I know it's crazy," she said, "but his eyes and his voice; ooh, it's so swoon worthy."

Ashley smirked. "He does have a certain mystique about him," she admitted. "That's for sure."

Amanda explained, "It's the mystery, along with everything else, that wants me to get to know him better."

Ashley patted her supervisor's hand "Look, Amanda, sweetie," she said. "I know some people buy into this whole 'love at first sight' stuff, but you have to remember, he works for you. Hank is a good worker, and I don't want us to lose him because he's suddenly caught your eye."

Amanda sat on the edge of her bed and let out a sigh. "You're right," she said. "I've only just met him. I don't know if he feels the same towards me."

"Your current feelings for Hank are based on an immediate attraction," Ashley explained. "My advice for you is to keep observing him from afar. That way, you can see there's a lot more to him than his face or his voice. Besides, the whole employer-employee relationship aspect is unprofessional, if not creepy. I don't want there to be some sort of sexual harassment suit filed against a member of Gerald's family because she got gooey over Hank Acker."

Amanda composed herself. "Alright then," she said, "I'll do that. Thanks for straightening me out, Ashley."

Ashley smiled. "Hey, we're the only women on this farm," she said. "We need to talk to our fellow sisters, on occasion. I want you to know if you ever need to chat about anything, I'm here for you."

"Thanks," Amanda said. "That offer goes for you, too. If you need to get anything off your chest, you can come to me."

"Much appreciated, Amanda," Ashley replied. "Shall we see how the boys are making out in the kitchen?"

"I think we should," Amanda stated. "Hopefully, they haven't flooded the place out."

Ashley laughed. "We'll find out if the bottom of the stairs is under water," she said.

~ * * * ~

The women headed back down to the kitchen. Upon entering, they saw the boys continuing to wash the pots and dishes. Hank did the scrubbing; while Cecil handled the rinsing, and Kevin dried and put them back in their cupboards. This brought a smile to Amanda's face.

"Thanks for doing the dishes, guys," said the heir. "Is there any way I can pack you in my luggage and take you back to Toronto with me? I can always use an extra set of hands at my place."

Cecil laughed. "I don't know about that, Amanda," he said. "We're all married to our job here."

Kevin added, "And the land doesn't take too kindly to us cheating on her."

Ashley chimed in, "That's good because I'll be damned if I let you three take off for Ontario, and leave me having to take care of the place all by myself."

"Don't worry, Ashley," Hank assured. "We all made a vow to Gerald not to turn our backs on this place, and we don't intend to renege on it."

"Especially," Kevin said, "if Amanda is going to help us out in getting funding to keep this place alive."

With the dishes done, the hired hands retired to their guest house to enjoy the rest of their evening. Ashley leaned over to Amanda and whispered, "I'm not sure if you're the type to be a 'Peeping Tammy,' but if you're interested, there's a prime view of Hank's bedroom window from the upstairs study. Just make sure you keep the curtains closed to conceal yourself. The prairie moon can be a bright one."

"Thanks for the tip," the supervisor replied.

With a wink, Ashley scooted off to her room, and Amanda headed to the den, so she could get further caught up on her work back in Toronto. The wireless signal was spotty in the farm house, but she did the best she could. "If I'm going to spend more time here," she thought, "I'm going to have to upgrade the service. But, that's something I'll take care of on my next visit."

~ * * * ~

Amanda was in mid-project when she heard a distinctive twang bellowing from the guest house.

"Are you guys done with the shower?" Hank asked. "If you are, I'm going to jump in right now."

Amanda was thankful she had left the window open to let in some fresh air, so she could catch the journeyman's query. She lowered the lid on her laptop, and scurried upstairs to stake out her observation post. Amanda made sure the curtains were pulled closed; save for a small crack to peer out of, and kept the lights of the study off. She didn't want Hank to see her while she was peering through his window. Amanda positioned one of the chairs near the window, so she could have a seat while she waited for his return. When he did, she was not disappointed.

She heard the faint click of a door opening, and leapt to the window to see if it was Hank returning to his room. Peering from her vantage point she saw him walking towards his window; clad in only a towel wrapped around his waist. Amanda had to duck out of view to make sure he didn't see her. Hank closed his open window, and walked away. When the coast was clear, she peeked from the opening between the curtains, and observed Hank in his almost-nude glory.

She thought, "Holy shit! Hank is one buff guy. Does Ashley know about this? If she did, I'm surprised she hasn't made a play for him yet."

Hank removed his towel, and Amanda had to stifle her gasp in amazement. The journeyman revealed himself to be a well endowed male. She figured he must have been ten inches when erect. The sight of Hank brought an immediate arousal to Amanda. She felt herself getting damp through her panties, and had the sudden urge for sexual release. Amanda carefully undid the fly to her pants, and slid her hand inside. Her arousal was confirmed as her fingertips made contact with the moist fabric. A soft moan escaped from her lips, as she started to massage herself through the material. Her free hand began to slowly unbutton her blouse; her torso wanting to breathe the moment in.

In Amanda's mind, she envisioned Hank taking her into his arms; holding her close with her breasts pressed against his muscular chest. She yearned for his touch, as Hank carried her over to the bed; Amanda's legs wrapped around his waist, as a symbol of not wanting to let him go. Amanda's hand slipped inside her panties, as she imagined Hank entering her. She let out a gasp as her fingers brushed against her nub, and began to lightly massage it. Her free hand cupped her breast; imagining his lips teasing her erect nipple. Then, Amanda allowed herself to slip a finger inside of her; bringing her closer to the pinnacle of ecstasy. She needed this, and she needed Hank. Her body ached for him to be making love to her at that moment; kissing, caressing, and stroking forth. Amanda wanted the waves of passion to wash over the both of them, and be swept away with each other.

She tried to make the sensation last for as long as possible.
However, with a silent moan for Hank, Amanda found herself
tumbling over the edge; releasing all of her erotic tension. Her
body quivered as the pulsating waves of her orgasm overtook her.
The feeling of bliss was powerful enough to have Amanda collapse
in her chair. Her flesh beaded with sweat; her breath was short and
laboured. When she regained her composure, Amanda redressed
for a short while before she got into her shower to wash the smell
of sex from her body. As she lathered herself up, she knew another
one of her missions: if given the opportunity, before she returned
to Toronto, she wanted to bed Hank Acker.

CHAPTER FIVE

When everyone gathered around the breakfast table the next morn, there was a smile on Amanda's face. She entered the dining room wearing a blue denim shirt and black jeans, accented with a wide white belt; basic attire on the farm, but with a hint of designer style to her ensemble. It was an outfit she hoped would garner compliments from her male staff. They did not disappoint her.

"You look nice, Amanda," Cecil complimented.

Kevin joked, "Did you do something to your hair?"

Amanda laughed and said, "It's just the wonders of a good night's sleep, guys."

Hank said, "There must be something magical about your bed, because you have a certain glow about you this morning."

If Hank knew what had transpired in the upstairs study the night before, he would've eaten his words. "I guess it must be the pure Saskatchewan air," Amanda said.

Ashley noticed Amanda's glow the minute she saw her. The female staff member leaned over to her new boss and whispered, "I take it you took advantage of my little spying tip last night."

Amanda nodded to her female counterpart with a wink. She sat down at the table and asked, "So, what's on the breakfast menu today, gang?"

Kevin answered, "It is Tuesday, so per our tradition, Cecil and Ashley whipped up a batch of pancakes for all of us."

Hank added, "And I ran into town and grabbed coffee for all of us from Timmy's. I didn't know how you liked yours, so I got you a double-double."

Amanda took the takeout cup from his hand. "Double-double is how I have it back home," she said. "Thank you, Hank. With this type of hospitality, I'm not sure if I would ever want to return to Toronto; I can get used to this."

Cecil passed his supervisor the platter of fluffy dough fresh from the griddle. "I hope you like these ones. We made them with Saskatoon berries."

"Oh, my God," Amanda exclaimed. "I haven't had Saskatoon berries in years! They're the one thing I've missed since I moved out east."

"They don't have them in Ontario?" Ashley asked.

"Some supermarkets do, but they are very hard to come by. Plus, they're not as fresh as they are here in Saskatchewan."

After placing a pad of butter and adding a light drizzle of syrup to her pancakes, Amanda dove in. Once the Saskatoon berries burst in her mouth, it brought back the memories of her youth. Amanda and Evelyn would go berry picking every summer, and they would bring back baskets of the robust purple-hued fruit. They would use the berries for homemade pancakes and baked goods. Evelyn's baking expertise was so renowned; she once won a local contest for her Saskatoon berry pie. Amanda let out a contented sigh, as she remembered the good times she had with her aunt.

Hank mentioned, "Pancakes and pies are wonderful, but I hear there's a restaurant in Calgary that serves a Saskatoon berry cheesecake."

Amanda and Ashley's eyes grew large. "Saskatoon berry cheesecake?!?" they asked in unison.

Cecil rolled his eyes. "Now you've done it, Hank," he said. "You know how some women get when you mention things like cheesecake or chocolate."

Ashley slapped her co-worker's arm. "Hush, you," she scolded. "We can't help it if we have a sweet tooth."

Amanda whispered to her partner-in-crime, "After the dream I had last night, I can envision a naughty scenario involving Hank, chocolate sauce, and whipped cream."

Ashley whispered back, "Damn, you're one kinky gal. Does the big city do that to every small town girl?"

Amanda giggled. "No," she whispered, "just me whenever I think about big, beefy guys like him. By the way, do you suppose we could have another girl talk after the boys are back out in the field?"

"Sure thing," Ashley said. "We can talk while we're in the kitchen doing the dishes."

Amanda turned her attention to the others. "Do you think you guys will be done planting the field today?" she asked.

Kevin mused, "That's hard to say. If the weather holds, we could be finished by late this afternoon. But, if there's any rain blowing in, it'll delay us another day or two."

Hank asked, "Do you think you can check the weather report on your laptop, Amanda?"

"I can try," she said, "but the wireless signal out here is spotty at best."

"That's probably because I was on the desktop last night playing my Facebook games," Cecil admitted.

Ashley admonished him. "Oh for the love of Pete, Cecil," she said. "Why in the blue hell are you playing that stupid computer farming game when you work on the real deal?"

"That's not the only game I play," Cecil replied. "There are a few trivia games I play on there, too."

Ashley sighed, and turned to her new boss. "Do you see what I've had to put up with, Amanda?" she asked. "Before you showed up, I had to be the voice of reason for these guys."

Hank objected to his counterpart's remark. "Hey," he said, "I'm not *that* bad."

"No, Hank," Ashley assured. "You're the most sensible one out of the three of you. Kevin's the smart ass and Cecil... well, God only knows about him."

"I love you too, Ashley," Cecil replied with a hint of sarcasm.

Amanda attempted to restore order. "Anyway," she said, "if one of you guys could fetch it from the den, I'd be glad to look it up for you."

Kevin stood up from the table. "I'll get it for you," he said, before rushing off to the front of the house. He returned with the portable computer and Amanda fired up the Environment Canada website.

"Looks like there's a 40% chance of rain this afternoon," she announced. "I hope it will hold off, so you guys can get your work done."

Cecil suggested, "If we're going to beat any chance of rain, we better get a move on."

Ashley said, "You guys run along. Amanda and I will clean up."

"Thanks, gals," Hank replied. "We don't know what we'd do without you."

Amanda whispered to Ashley, "After my dream last night, I know what he could do to me."

The female staff member rolled her eyes, but stifled a giggle in the process.

~ * * * ~

The girls made sure the guys left the house before heading into the kitchen to get started on the dishes.

Ashley said, "So, you look like you saw quite a show last night."

"Did I ever," Amanda confessed. "I caught Hank coming out of the shower, and he is quite a specimen."

"He sure is," Ashley agreed. "I remember when he first started working here; I was going through the same trepidations as you are right now."

The heir said, "I'm going to take a stab in the dark here and guess you've previously utilized the upstairs study for your viewing pleasure, right?"

Ashley laughed. "I'd be lying if I said I didn't," she said. "Hank's certified Grade-A Canadian beefcake, and I'm happy we have him in our little fold."

"That brings me to my next question," Amanda probed. "If you've known him longer, has anyone tried to make a play for him?"

"Amanda honey, there have been a few women who've come by here; trying to saddle up with that man, but he's too much bronco for a filly to handle."

"We're talking about what he's packing between his legs, right?"

Ashley laughed again. "Believe me," she said, "I wanted to sample his 'smoked meat log' when I first saw it, too. But, because Hank and I work together, I didn't want to complicate things. I valued the friendship he and I share more than a romp in the hayloft, and so should you. You're going on about how much you'd want to frolic with him, but you're forgetting that he still works *for* you. We're in enough legal trouble as it is with Rebecca. You don't want to add a sexual harassment lawsuit to the court docket, do you?"

Amanda weighed Ashley's words with caution. She was finding herself in the same position her confidante was in. If she decided to enter a relationship with Hank, it could jeopardize things around the farm. Would things still be harmonious between the two of them, let alone the other employees, if things didn't work out? Would Hank even stick around? He might decide he couldn't work for someone who was always hitting on him, and move on to the next stop on his itinerary. Amanda had to play her cards right, as not to lose the respect of the other workers. However, she wanted to be with Hank. She felt a tingling sensation at the thought of being in his embrace; feeling his rugged lips pressed against hers.

If it wasn't for Ashley handing her another plate to dry, Amanda might have conducted a repeat performance from the night before.

"You're thinking about him again, aren't you?" Ashley asked.

"I can't help it," Amanda admitted. "Part of me is telling me to resist, but the other half is overcome with my raging hormones. I don't know what to do."

Ashley put down her scouring brush, and turned to her boss. "Let me ask you something," she said, "when was the last time you were with a man?"

The question shocked Amanda. She had not heard of such boldness from an employee to her employer before, let alone anything involving herself. It was blunt, but forced her to be honest with herself.

Amanda sighed and confessed. "If truth be told," she said, "I haven't had much of a chance to date anyone because of my job. I've been so wrapped up in my career; I haven't had any time for a relationship."

Ashley thought for a second. "Hmm," she said, "perhaps this is your mind telling you it's time to settle down with someone. You're in, what, your late-20s, or early-30s? Maybe it's telling you your chance for having a child is running out, and it needs to act quickly before the opportunity is lost."

There it was; the one thing that had been buried deep in the back of Amanda's mind. She knew one day she wanted to have children, but she preferred to have been established in her career before bringing a new life into the world. Alas, her career had been hectic as of late, and she didn't have an opportunity to meet someone to spend the rest of her life with, and be the father of her child.

Amanda felt if she didn't act soon, her chance to be a mother would pass her by. Yes, there was still time for it all, but the added responsibility of being the owner of Gerald's farm threw her mind into frenzy.

Perhaps, this was the reason her eyes caught Hank. He looked like the ideal mate for her. His rugged good looks appealed to her at first, but when she saw him in all of his naked glory, her physical attraction towards him was added into the mix. However, it was all she had at the present. Save for some basics about his past, Amanda had no idea what type of person Hank could be. For all she knew, he could be an egotistical jerk who had no respect for women. It was a mystery that confounded Amanda, but she wanted to find out what made him tick. It was the only way she could know for certain if Hank was indeed Mr. Right.

Amanda asked, "You've known him for longer than I have. What sort of things is he into? What type of music does he like? Does he read or watch TV?"

Ashley giggled, "You really want to pursue this, don't you?"

"I am intrigued by the prospect," the heir admitted. "Come on, Ashley, throw me a bone here."

Ashley smirked. "That's strange," she said. "After seeing what you saw, I thought you wanted him to bone you."

Amanda smacked her cohort's arm with the dish towel. "Now, who's the naughty one of us?" she said. "But seriously, how can I get Hank to notice me?"

"Alright, for the sake of argument, let's say this won't cause any problems. Let's pick your brain for what you would do. If Hank lived in Toronto, and you wanted to ask him out, what would you propose for a first meeting?"

Amanda thought for a minute, and responded, "I guess I'd ask him out for a coffee. Do people go on coffee dates out here?"

Ashley laughed. "Yeah, we do," she said. "Although, when the only coffee shop around here is the Timmy's, and this being a small town; you know the whole town will hear about it in due time."

"That will make it a challenge," Amanda noted. "I want this to be discreet, and not get back to certain others."

"You mean Kevin and Cecil, right?" Ashley asked.

"Exactly," Amanda replied, "you saw how they noticed right away when I was daydreaming about Hank. I don't want them to give either of us a hard time because we're on what might be classed as a date."

"Amanda, sweetie," the staff member said, "they're going to find out sooner or later, and chances are they will both make a big deal out of it, unprofessional or not. That's how some guys are, but should they start on either one of you, I'll tell them to knock it off."

"Thanks, Ashley," Amanda said. "I appreciate it."

Ashley patted Amanda's hand. "Hey," she said, "someone's got to be the 'sensible one' around here. I'm hoping with you around it'll lighten that load for me, but I think I'll be taking on the role for a while longer."

The women finished the dishes, and Ashley headed off to the barn to commence the rest of her daily chores. Amanda got back to work on her project for the office back in Toronto, but the whole time, she was concocting her plan to get some alone time with Hank. She wanted to establish a foundation before they went out as a group on Friday night. If Amanda was going to pull it off, she had to put her plan into action as soon as possible. She came to a conclusion: she'd make her move just after dinner tomorrow night.

CHAPTER SIX

The next day drew on with patchy clouds rolling along the prairie sky. The rain wasn't able to hold off for Wednesday, but the skies cleared the following morning; thus, enabling the boys to get their work done out in the fields. Ashley was occupied with getting the processing equipment ready in advance of the harvest later on in the season. Meanwhile, Amanda kept busy by working on her laptop, trying to do some virtual legwork in a bid to receive financial assistance so she could pay the farm's bills. However, once again, her mind had wandered off to her thoughts about Hank. She conjured up the mental image of him, shirtless, coming into the house from working hard in the fields; the Saskatchewan summer sun beating down upon him. He'd grab a bottle of water before stepping back onto the porch and dousing himself with the clear liquid, the droplets cascading over his muscular torso in a scene which got Amanda's temperature rising. She was becoming lost in her daydream again, but was awakened by the ringing of the phone.

"Hello, Amanda," a familiar female voice spoke. "I hope I'm not disturbing you."

Amanda recognized the voice of Leonard's wife. "Not at all, Linda," she said. "What's going on?"

"Leonard wanted me to call you to see how you're making out on the farm," Linda probed.

"Financially, things are a mess, but you know that already. Other than that, things are going along great," Amanda stated. "The guys are hoping to finish the seeding within the next couple of days, so

---

we'll have this year's crop in the ground, and Ashley is getting the barn ready for when it comes time for harvest. So, other than the money issues, everything's going smoothly."

"Are you not having much luck contacting the local Member of Parliament?" Linda asked.

Amanda sighed. "Unfortunately not," she said. "I've tried sending emails to him, but I haven't gotten any response. I might have to go the Saskatchewan Ministry of Agriculture branch office in Yorkton, or the main offices in Regina to rattle their cages and see if we can get some help."

"I hope you're successful," Linda said. "I'd hate for your uncle's farm to end that way. But enough depressing stuff, how is everyone treating you out there?"

"We all get along great," Amanda replied. "I've found a good confidante in Ashley, and we've had a couple of girl talks already."

Linda's voice became inquisitive. "Oh, yeah?" she asked. "What have you been talking about?"

Amanda attempted to play coy. "Oh, you know," she said, "the 'scenery' out here."

Linda didn't miss a beat. "Yeah," she noted, "that Hank is quite a piece of eye candy, isn't he?"

Amanda's jaw dropped. Apparently, she and Ashley were not the only women who knew of the journeyman's attractiveness. She asked, "He's caught your eye too?"

"I have," Linda admitted. "Hank Acker has to be the hottest guy in all of Melville, so it's natural for a woman to ogle him."

"Does Leonard know you've been doing that?" Amanda asked.

"He doesn't," Linda said, "and I swear, Amanda, you tell him that I have been…"

The heir laughed. "Relax, Linda," she reassured. "Your secret is safe with me."

Linda composed herself. "Anyway," she said, "I was wondering if you'd like to meet up for coffee later."

Amanda cringed. "Can I take a rain check on that?" she asked. "I was hoping Hank and I could go out for coffee and a chat tonight."

Linda was shocked. "You're going to make a play for him tonight, huh?" she asked. "You do know the possible headaches behind such a move, right?"

"I do," Amanda assured, "but it's nothing like that. I just wanted to go out, and find out more about him."

"Don't lie to me, Amanda," Linda scolded. "Do the others know about this proposed 'date'?"

"It's not a 'date', per se," Amanda corrected, "but only Ashley, and now, you, know about it. I'm hoping both of you will keep it quiet, but I'm worried about how Kevin and Cecil might act when they find out."

"I'm sure Hank will keep them in line," Linda said.

"I hope so, too," the heir added. "Ashley said she'll intervene if they get out of control, and you know Ashley's the type who doesn't take shit from anybody."

Leonard's wife laughed. "Neither does Hank," she said. "He looks like he's been in a few rodeos himself."

The two women chatted for a while longer. Amanda said she would try to make it out to Linda and Leonard's place the next day because little Nate wanted to see his cousin from the big city. It was a promise which appealed to Linda because the two women had not had an opportunity to talk since Amanda relocated to the farm. After saying their goodbyes, Amanda headed to the kitchen to start working on that night's dinner: pork chops with mini potatoes and a vegetable medley.

~ * * * ~

The boys came in from the fields early, and grabbed their showers. Amanda was tempted to head back to the upstairs study to get another eyeful of Hank, but had to keep an eye on the stove. Ashley arrived from the barn, and asked if she could help out. As they were setting the table, they went over Amanda's plan: she would ask to speak with Hank alone after dinner, and make her pitch for the coffee meeting then. Amanda figured if she did it alone, it would avoid the mocking of the other guys. The guys entered the dining room, and everyone sat down to enjoy the meal.

Amanda commented, "I saw you guys come in early. Are the fields all seeded?"

Kevin said, "Yep, the whole corn crop has been planted. It's safe for the rain to come in now; our work's done for the next little while."

Ashley noted, "Excellent, now you guys can help me out in the barn. It hasn't been easy trying to work on the processor alone."

48

Cecil attempted to defend, "But, you're so good at it. We're afraid we'd only get in the way."

"That is bullshit," Ashley scolded, "and you know it. You guys would rather get your necessary Vitamin D while we women are slaving away indoors."

Cecil continued to plead his case. "That's not true," he said. We wouldn't know which nut or bolt would go where. It's not a matter of 'Insert Tab A into Slot B.'"

Ashley called his bluff. "Oh, like you would know anything about inserting things into a slot, Cecil," she said. "Take that for any way you want."

Amanda giggled at Ashley's innuendo. She was enjoying the banter between her female counterpart and the guys, but she was starting to grow nervous about what was to come. Would Hank be receptive of her proposal? Would he even take her up on the offer? She was eager for the dinner to end, so she could ask Hank out. However, she had to be patient and let things run their natural course.

Dinner continued on, and everyone discussed their upcoming soiree in a week's time. It was agreed it would be a good chance for everybody to unwind after a week's work. Kevin suggested the guys should hit the bar and have a beer to celebrate the end of planting. If there was a chance for Amanda to make her move, now was the time.

"Actually Hank," she interrupted, "after you and the guys are done with the dishes, could I speak with you privately for a moment?"

"Am I in trouble?" he asked.

Cecil mocked, "Uh oh, Hank's in the dog house. Did you use the toilet upstairs and forget to put the seat down?" The quip earned a smack from Ashley.

"It's not that at all," Amanda said. "There's something I need to discuss with him one-on-one."

Kevin pondered aloud, "You want a private conversation with Hank, and he's not in trouble? The plot thickens."

"Mind your own beeswax, you two," Ashley threatened.

"Sure thing, Amanda," Hank replied. "I'll meet with you in the den after we're done in the kitchen."

Amanda did her best to hide her smile. "That would be greatly appreciated," she said.

~ * * * ~

The meal ended, and the boys started to clear the table. Ashley and Amanda went into the den and talked about what was about to happen.

"Are you nervous?" Ashley asked.

"A little, but I need to be assertive. I don't want it to come off like I'm throwing myself at him."

"Just be yourself, and say you didn't get much of a chance to talk to him with everybody around. Tell him you found his back story interesting, and would like to hear more about it. That way, you might possibly avoid any blowback should he feel uncomfortable about the situation."

"But," Amanda asked, "what if he sees right through it, and shoots me down? Or worse, he files a lawsuit against me?"

"He might, or he might not," Ashley said. "You won't know for certain until you play your cards. The way I see it, if you don't play them in the right sequence, it would be an opportunity lost, and some other broad will try to make a play for him, and you'll end up in court for something other than Rebecca's suit."

While Amanda needed to be sensible about the whole situation, the thought of another woman coming onto Hank repulsed Amanda. Yes, he was an attractive man, and women were bound to throw themselves at him. He could have his pick of any woman he wanted, but she knew none of them had been successful as of yet. This was the glimmer of hope Amanda held onto. Perhaps she would be the one to break through the line and capture Hank's heart. But, she had to throw caution to the wind, and take the first step in doing so.

A few minutes later, Hank entered the den. "You wanted to speak with me, Amanda?" he asked.

"I'll leave you two alone," Ashley commented before leaving the room. Once the two of them were alone, Amanda made her pitch.

The heir took a deep breath. "I'm sorry to have called you out during dinner tonight," she said, "but I wanted to speak with you alone without being accosted by the others."

"Yeah, Kevin and Cecil can be a bit immature at times," Hank said, "so what's on your mind?"

Amanda chose her words carefully. "Well, I know Kevin suggested you guys go out for a beer tonight," she said, "but I was wondering if you would like to go out for coffee instead."

"Will it be all of us?" he asked.

"Nope," she said, "it'll be just you and me."

Hank blinked. "You mean like a date?" he asked.

"No, it's not a date at all," she lied. "I just found your story about your travelling around the Prairies fascinating, and I would like to hear more about it. But, I'd rather listen to it without Kevin and Cecil turning it into a mockery of you."

"What about Ashley?" Hank asked. "Wouldn't she be left all alone here?"

"I'll tell her she can go out with the other guys," Amanda said, "if she wants. Heck, if someone has to keep those two in line; it might as well be her."

"You have a point," Hank said. He thought about his new boss' request, and after a few moments, gave his answer. "Alright then," he said, "we'll go out for coffee together. Do you want me to meet you back here later?"

"We can go now if you'd like," she suggested.

"The chores have been done for the day," Hank stated, "we can go now. I have no problem with that."

Amanda fought to contain her excitement. "Great," she said, "just give me a moment to tell Ashley about your suggestion of chaperoning the boys. I'll meet you out by my car."

"Okay, then," he said. "I'll see you in a few."

~ * * * ~

Amanda walked towards the guest house, but she might have been walking on air for the short jaunt. She knocked on the door, and when Ashley answered, the female staffer was curious to know.

"So, what's the verdict?" she asked.

Amanda stifled a squeal. "He said, 'yes'," she reported.

"That's wonderful," Ashley replied. "You're going to have to tell me all about it when you get back."

Amanda composed herself and spoke in a normal tone. "I'm going out for a while," she said, "so if you'd like, you could go into town with the boys, and have a drink with them."

Picking up on the cue, Ashley played along. "Sure thing, Amanda," she replied. "It'll give me a chance to make sure they behave themselves." A faint groan came from upstairs; a clear sign Kevin and Cecil heard her. Ashley leaned towards Amanda and whispered, "Good luck, and be careful."

"Thanks for the vote of confidence," the heir whispered back.

Amanda headed back to the farm house, grabbed her purse, and met up with Hank at her car. She had completed the first step in "Operation: Acquire Acker," and hoped the next phase of her mission would be as successful.

CHAPTER SEVEN

The two co-workers entered the coffee shop and quickly found a table. Amanda suggested to Hank since he had bought the last round, she would treat him to the night's beverages. Hank appreciated the gesture, and asked for a double-double decaf. Amanda opted for some Apple Cinnamon tea with two sugars and three shots of milk. When the heir settled back at the table with the drinks, the employee made a confession.

"I have to admit," Hank said, "I'm a little hesitant about this outing."

"I can see why you'd be concerned," Amanda said. "A boss and her employee going out for coffee alone together; it smacks of possible sexual harassment. But, I assure you, Hank, I have no ulterior motives here tonight." Amanda checked outside the window to make sure there were no storm clouds on the horizon; fortunately for her, it was a moonlit night with minimal cloud cover.

Hank relaxed a little bit; however, the ensuing line of questioning made him wonder if he could take his supervisor at face value.

Amanda started her interview. "Now," she said, "when we were all doing our introductions during our first dinner together, you mentioned you were originally from Alberta?"

"Yes, Grande Prairie to be exact," Hank said. "I spent most of my youth there, but when I turned 18; my dad threw me out of the house. He said he didn't want me loafing around once I finished high school. So, I started travelling around the Prairies on my own."

"You couldn't afford to go to college?" she asked.

"Not really," he replied. "I had applied to attend Grande Prairie Regional, but they said my grades weren't good enough to get in. My dad said I should go get a job, but I grew tired of the whole retail sector. So, since I wasn't contributing to the household, he tossed me out on my ass."

"I'm sorry to hear that," Amanda stated. "Have you ever thought about getting into modeling?"

Hank rolled his eyes. "Oh sure, Amanda," he said. "Some agency would hire a guy with no money to buy the portfolio shots."

"I'm serious, Hank," she said. "You have the facial qualities where you could get hired by one." Then, thought to herself, "And, a hot body to match."

Hank became a little agitated. "I don't know," he answered in a stern tone. "I'm rather happy where I am now on the farm. And let me just say, I'm uncomfortable with such a suggestion."

Amanda had been found out. Hank could tell she was being unprofessional with her fact-finding mission. She didn't want to be in further legal hot water, not with Rebecca's challenge waiting in the wings. Amanda had to think fast to save face.

"I'm sorry, Hank," she apologized. "That was out of line of me. It's just, I was checking the farm's financial statements earlier, and I'm surprised we're still afloat."

"Is it that serious?" Hank asked.

Amanda fiddled with her half-empty cup. "Pretty much," she said. "I'm still looking into trying to get some financial assistance for the place, but I'm worried we might get turned down. You know how government departments can be."

The heir sighed, and Hank saw the look of sorrow on her face. Things looked bleak for the family business, and Amanda worried it might be too little and too late. Hank closed his eyes, took a deep breath, and made his offer.

"You know," he said, "I think I can find a way to help keep the farm alive for a little while longer."

Amanda was astonished at Hank's suggestion. "You can?" she asked. "How is that possible?"

"Don't worry about it," he insisted. "I'll talk to someone, and see if they can provide us with a short-term loan."

Amanda smiled. "If you could do that," she said, "that would be greatly appreciated. But, I don't know what we could offer as collateral."

"Leave that to me," Hank said. "I don't want you to give up the place. I want to make sure the others don't lose their jobs and home."

"Thanks, Hank," Amanda replied. "I know this is just a temporary solution, and I know we'll be able to turn things around. I'm just glad you're offering to help out with this." She took a sip from her coffee, and her nerves calmed. The heir hesitated about proceeding her original questioning, but did so with caution. "So," she asked, "tell me about some of the other places you've worked in the past, as you were travelling from town-to-town."

Hank recollected, "Well, I've worked on an oil rig up in Fort McMurray."

"That's a booming industry right now with the Oil Sands," Amanda noted. "Why did you leave there?"

"It was mostly a health issue. While the pay was good there, the long hours and dangerous work were taking a toll on my body. I wanted something with a little slower pace."

"Did you work elsewhere before coming to work for my uncle?"

"Yep, I've helped out on a cattle farm near Pincher Creek, played the team mascot for the junior hockey team in Medicine Hat, and drove a truck along the Trans-Canada between Calgary and Winnipeg, and all stops in between."

"That's quite a resume you've amassed," Amanda remarked.

Hank took a sip from his coffee cup. "It's a diverse work history, I do admit," he said, "but it wasn't until I pulled into Melville, and was hired on by Gerald, where I felt like staying in one place for a prolonged period. I guess it was God's way of saying it was time for me to settle down once and for all."

"A fact I'm sure my uncle was thankful for."

"As are Kevin, Cecil, and Ashley; the four of us together make a great team."

"Can I make an observation?" Amanda asked.

Hank retorted, "You're not planning on hitting on me again, are you?"

The heir laughed. "No," she said, "it's not that. I just wanted to say that for someone who couldn't afford college, you're quite an articulate man. I'm presuming you're self-taught?"

The employee nodded. "I spent my days off hanging out in libraries," he said. "I wanted to build my vocabulary in case I wanted to become something more than a labourer. Unfortunately, the opportunity never came. Most places want a certain level of education and so much experience, qualities I don't possess. But, I didn't want to be completely left behind, so I would go to the local library, do some reading, cross-reference the dictionaries and thesaurus for words I didn't quite understand, and built up my linguistic capabilities that way."

Amanda was impressed over such a factoid. It showed Hank was not only a hard worker physically, but mentally, as well. It earned a new level of admiration from her. "That's quite commendable," she said.

"Thank you," he replied. "So, we've talked about me; tell me about you. I know you're a graduate of the University of Saskatchewan and moved to Toronto to become an advertising executive. Is there anything else behind the woman who is Amanda Bellamy?"

"There isn't anything else beyond that," she said.

Hank persisted. "Oh, come on now," he said. "There has to be more to you than your education and job. Do you have any interests: sports, music, movies, or books?"

"I'm not really much of a sports fan; although, I will watch the odd hockey game. My music tastes lean towards Top 40 with some alternative thrown in. When it comes to movies I like a good drama. I find the whole rom-com genre to be corny. However, I do enjoy a nice romance book. Then again, what woman doesn't? What about you?"

"I'm more of a rock-and-roll guy when it comes to music," Hank admitted, "but I do like some of today's Top 40; just none of this bubble gum-pop crap. Movie-wise, I go into dramas and comedies, and I agree with you on the rom-com stuff. Of course, if I'm out on a date, and my companion suggests we go see one, I'll do my best to stomach the film."

Amanda smirked. "I'm sure you've been to your share of those," she commented.

Hank was confused. "What do you mean?" he asked.

Amanda chose her words carefully. She reasoned, "I'm just saying a good looking guy, like you, has probably been on quite a few dates with the women around town."

"Can I let you in on a little something, Amanda?"

Her heart began to sink, fearing the worst. "Sure thing, Hank," she said. "Don't think of me as your boss, but as your friend."

Hank leaned in and said in a low tone, "I've had quite a few women in this town hit on me."

Amanda's hopes brightened a bit; however, she was still cautious. "Have all of their advances made you uncomfortable?" she asked.

"A little," he said. "The problem is, when I'm on a date with them, I find we have little in common. Plus, I get the vibe they want to do unspeakable things to me, and I'm not that type of guy."

"What type of guy is that?"

Hank explained, "You know, the type of guy who women want a romp in the sack with. I don't mind flirting suggestively with them, but I prefer to establish a meaningful relationship that goes beyond the modern social constructs of sex. I blame the latest string of contemporary adult novels for destroying the sanctity of pure romance as I know it."

"It is a shame the genre has altered the view of traditional romance," Amanda said, "but most women find it appealing. However, I do understand where you're coming from. Today's romance novels are all about animalistic sex. Gone are the days of traditional courtship where guys would do their best to woo a woman. Now, it's all 'pin them up against the wall, rip off each other's clothes, and get at it.' There's passion, but no seduction. It's become a lost art."

Hank agreed. "Exactly," he said, "if women are into that, all the more power to them. But, that's not the type of guy I am. I'll give you an example: say I wanted to enter into a relationship with you. I would ask you out, we'd go out on a few dates, get to know one another, and hope we'd fall in love with one another that way. Only then, when we both truly in love with each other would I pursue the intimacy option. Nowadays, they're more into lust-ridden passion without any real romance. It just appears hollow to me."

Amanda was surprised by Hank's openness. She blushed at the idea of the journeyman trying to romance a woman, and wished he might turn his sights on her one day. Originally, she was interested in getting him in between the sheets; however, after hearing Hank explain his approach to relationships, he showed an endearing quality. Some men appeared to be interested in putting notches in their bedpost instead of pursuing a long-term commitment. Hank was one to break the mould where he had an appearance that would cause any woman's panties to drop; yet, didn't possess any of the macho bravado that stereotypically came with it. He was a man with a deeper layer, and Amanda was thankful she received an opportunity to see it during the outing.

Amanda said, "Could I be bold to ask what it is you're looking for in a woman? We've established you're not fond of the ones who throw themselves at you for a night or two of meaningless sex."

Hank shrugged. "I don't know," he said. "I guess I like a woman who has a sense of humour, a great conversationalist, and isn't all hung up about the materialistic things in life. I prefer a woman who is down to Earth, and is not consumed with her career, or the idea of getting married and having kids by a certain age. I don't mind if they have certain goals, but I feel if they're too ambitious to meet certain deadlines, it could harm the relationship."

Amanda's original train of thought stopped dead in its tracks. Hearing the words come out of Hank's mouth made the heir evaluate how she was going to pursue the blond-haired hunk sitting across from her. Yes, her biological clock was ticking, but was it that pressing to settle down and start a family? Amanda had turned 30 a couple of months before, so she still had plenty of time left before she could become a loving wife and mother. But, what about what he said about being 'consumed with her career?'

Yes, Amanda brought her laptop with her to Melville in order to work on her advertising campaigns for Mr. Lawrence back in Toronto. However, it was because she was still tied to her original profession. If she were to stand a chance with Hank, would she have to sacrifice everything she had worked for the past five years since moving away from Saskatchewan? Was this fate's way of telling her she should return home to the Prairies, and settle down in the province where she grew up? Toronto had afforded her so many opportunities, but none of them involved what was sitting across from her inside the Timmy's.

Hank asked, "Since you asked me, what about you? What qualities in a guy catch your eye?"

Amanda snapped back to reality. She answered, "Well, I'll admit being physically attractive is what will get my attention to start. Beyond that, I'd have to say he'd have to be a guy who could make me laugh, would support me in anything I would do – much like I'd support him in anything he did – but, wouldn't judge me if I proved myself to be human, and made the odd mistake; unless it was a big one. In which case, I'd hope he'd understand, and we'd work through it together. He would be comfortable with going out for a night on the town; as much as he would with spending the night in, curled up together on the couch while watching a movie."

Hank chuckled. "Sounds like you're a bit of a hopeless romantic yourself," he noted.

Amanda blushed. "In some aspects, I am," she confessed, "but, I have to admit, I don't get much of an opportunity to go out on dates, or spend time with that special someone."

"Life must be tough in the world of advertising," he observed.

"Work keeps me busy most of the time," she said, "but there are some nights where I want to stay home, and curl up with a good book."

"You would think there would be guys clamouring to ask you out."

Amanda smirked, "I don't think I'm anything to write home about."

"Nonsense," Hank disputed. "If I may be candid enough to say it, you're an attractive woman, yourself. I can understand if you feel hesitant because I'm sure there are a bunch of hounds in a city like

Toronto. But, I think if the right man came along, you'd be quite a catch for him."

Amanda blushed at Hank's compliment. While she didn't think she wasn't special, he thought she was 'attractive'; earning him brownie points in the process. Amanda brushed her auburn hair away from her emerald eyes, and smiled. They were sparkling in the light of the coffee shop; a fact not lost on Hank.

"I hope I don't get reprimanded for this, but has anybody ever complimented you on your beautiful eyes?" he asked.

Amanda laughed. "Now, who's sexually harassing who?" she said.

"I'm sorry if I crossed the line," he apologized.

"It's alright," she reassured. "My eyes are what they are. I never thought much about them."

Amanda looked up from her cup, and caught a similar sparkle from her date's eyes. The setting sun from outside, combined with the lights inside the coffee shop brought out the blue from Hank's irises. They appeared to be two shimmering pools, and Amanda was becoming lost in them. She had to look away before she tipped her hand to him.

Hank asked, "Is there something wrong?"

"No, it's just..." Amanda's words trailed off. She was trying to find the right thing to say, so she didn't come across like a love-struck girl who got the courage to speak to her crush for the first time. She took a deep breath and apologized, "I'm sorry. My mind is all over the place tonight. This is the first time I've had a chance to get out of the house since I moved in on Sunday. I've been going a little stir-crazy with everything that's gone on, and now I've had the opportunity to sit down and talk, I'm having problems formulating the right words to say."

Hank took Amanda's hand in his and comforted her. "You still miss your uncle, don't you?" he asked.

Amanda sighed. "I'd be lying if I said I didn't think about him every day," she said. "I'm thankful he bequeathed me the farm; it's given me the opportunity to meet the great people who worked for him. I'm just worried about what will happen when I have to return to my normal life in Toronto. I don't want things to go down the toilet after I'm gone."

"Don't worry, Amanda," Hank said. "You're doing an amazing job being there with us the past few days. It's been difficult to adjust to life post-Gerald, but we've been able to pull together, and we're making sure the farm stays alive. As long as we're all able to lean on one another, we'll get through this."

"I sure hope so, Hank. I don't want the farm to fall into disrepair, or worse: fall into the hands of my cousin, Rebecca."

"The lawyer will make sure it doesn't come to that. Gerald had a good head on his shoulders, and he wouldn't have left the farm to you unless he knew it would be in the hands of someone he trusted."

Amanda relaxed to his employee's encouraging words. "You're right, Hank," she said, "thanks. I don't want to let him down, and as long as I have you, Ashley, and the other guys helping out, we'll make it work."

Hank checked his watch. "It's getting late," he noted. "We should head back."

"Yes, we should," she said, "although, we might be the only ones there. I hope Ashley's been making sure Kevin and Cecil behave."

"Ashley can crack a mean whip when she wants to. Besides, I think she wants to make sure they're admitted back to the bar for our little night out-cum-memorial on Friday night."

"Yes, it would suck if we had to hold it elsewhere because those two couldn't hold their liquor."

"Not to mention all of the backtalk we'd get from the town because of their perceived behaviour. Gerald was an upstanding man in the community, and he'd roll over in his grave if anyone tarnished his reputation."

The two finished their drinks and drove back to the farm. When they pulled up, Amanda didn't see any lights on at the guest house, and presumed Ashley and the others were still in town. Hank walked her up to the main house's front door, like the gentleman he was.

Amanda said, "Thank you for the night out, Hank. I really needed it tonight."

"It was my pleasure," Hank said, "although in fairness, you were the one who asked me out."

"Yes, I did," she replied, "but thank you for the company. I enjoyed our conversation tonight. It's given me a lot to think about."

Hank was surprised. "Oh," he asked, "anything in particular?"

Amanda giggled. "Now, Hank," she said, "a girl has to have some secrets."

"Fair enough; thank you for the evening, and I wish you a good night," he replied, and turned to leave.

Amanda interrupted, "Hank, wait."

He stopped in his tracks at the bottom of the porch steps and turned towards her. Amanda walked towards him, and looked into his eyes. The prairie moon shone down on both of them, and illuminated their irises with a romantic twinkle. Amanda stood on her tiptoes, and kissed Hank upon his cheek.

"Thank you, again," she replied. "I couldn't end the evening without a good night kiss."

"Oh, how rude of me," Hank apologized. "Here I am, giving you the impression of being a gentleman, and I forgot about the key component to the end of any date. If it's not too late, may I?"

Hank caressed Amanda's cheek, looked into her sparkling green eyes, and leaned in for a tender kiss. While she had kissed him on his cheek, Amanda was surprised when his lips met hers. They were rough to the touch, but the kiss was soft and sweet. It sent a charge throughout her body, but she didn't pull away. Amanda wrapped her arms around the back of his neck to support her as she melted into the kiss. There was a romantic feel to it with a subtle hint of passion, but nothing that would lead her to believe there would be more to come once they broke away. Hank backed away, and helped Amanda settle the soles of her feet back on the ground.

"I'll see you in the morning," he smiled.

A breathless Amanda nodded, "See you in the morning."

Hank entered the guest house and shut the door behind him. Amanda slowly walked back up to the main house and entered the premises. When she closed the door behind her, she exhaled with a wistful sigh. She could get used to being kissed by Hank on a regular basis. The electricity that coursed through her body when his lips met hers was unlike anything she had felt before. It made her yearn for more, but she knew she would have to keep it a secret for now; at least, until Ashley came back from her night out.

~ * * * ~

Amanda was about to turn in for the night when the knock came at the door downstairs. There was only one person who would have bothered to disturb her at this hour, but given what had transpired earlier, she knew she was about to be interrogated. Amanda retied the strap to her robe and trudged down the stairs. When she opened the door, she found Ashley standing in front of her in an excited frenzy.

"I was wondering when you were going to show up," Amanda said.

Ashley whispered, "I had to sneak out of the guest house, so I wouldn't wake the boys. I saw your car in the driveway when we got back, and I couldn't wait until the morn to find out how things went."

Amanda ushered her gal pal into the den, and quietly closed the front door behind her.

Ashley demanded, "So, I want to know all of the details, and don't leave anything out."

"Okay," Amanda stated, "as you know, we went into town for coffee, and Hank and I talked about various things."

"Was there anything juicy in particular?" Ashley probed.

"I don't know if you would call it juicy, but we did talk about what he looked for in a woman."

"And, what exactly might that be?"

Amanda told Ashley what Hank told her earlier in the evening: how he was into the traditional sense of romance compared to the lust-ridden ideas she had going into the meeting. Ashley and Amanda swooned at the thought of a man like Hank trying to woo a woman with dating and spending time together instead of passion-filled sex; although, they believed sex with a man like Hank would be awe-inspiring. They presumed it would showcase an erotic intensity; along with a tenderness that would make a woman know she is loved, and his devotion to her would never waver. It would be something that could only be dreamed of in the popular romance novels of yore, but would become a reality with him.

Ashley asked, "Did anything happen when the two of you got back here?"

"To be honest," Amanda said, "there wasn't anything special. He walked me to the front door downstairs like a true gentleman, and we said good night."

"That's it? No kiss good night? Not that it would've been professional."

"Actually, as he turned to leave, I chased after him, and gave him a peck on the cheek. That's when he clued in about it, and gave me one at the bottom of the porch steps."

Ashley smirked. "So much for professionalism," she said. "Now, you know I'm going to ask, but how was it?"

"My God, Ashley," Amanda explained, "it was everything I could have ever imagined. It was romantic, tender, and purely electric. I still get goose bumps just thinking about it."

Ashley's jaw dropped at the revelation. "Damn girl," she remarked, "you're one lucky lady. I've often wondered what it would be like to be kissed by him. Hearing you describe it makes me envious of you."

Amanda giggled. "As I'm sure a few other women around here have, too," she said. "I have to confide something with you, though. I knew going in he probably saw me as his boss and friend, but after that kiss, I'm starting to wonder if he sees there is something more than that."

"Has he given you any indication he might be interested in being more than friends?" Ashley asked. "You know, aside from the kiss."

"He did compliment me on my eyes," the heir replied.

"That's a start. What else have you got?"

"He said I was beautiful," Amanda continued, "and I 'would be a catch for any guy who fell for me.' He understood there were a bunch of creeps in a big city like Toronto; hence, why I would be hesitant. But, he believed those types of men wouldn't appreciate me for who I am."

Ashley mused, "If I didn't know any better, I'd say he was trying to charm himself into your heart; if not, your panties."

"Believe me," Amanda said, "I've heard all of the lame pick-up lines before, but for some reason, hearing it come from Hank's lips makes it sound more sincere; more genuine."

"Maybe he noticed you were feeling down on yourself, and was trying to be like a good friend. Hank sounds like the type of guy who could lift anyone's spirits."

Amanda rubbed her arm. "Perhaps," she said. "I just wish there was another way I could find out where he stood with me. I like the idea of him being there as someone I could lean on, but if he is interested in being more than 'just friends', I wouldn't push him away from it either."

Ashley patted her boss' hand. "Amanda, sweetie," she said, "this is Hank Acker we're talking about here. I don't think any woman would push him away if he showed an interest in them. If anything, they'd probably lead him upstairs to their bedroom for some serious one-on-one time."

"Be it as it may, could you imagine spending a night all curled up in his arms? I bet it would feel like heaven."

Ashley laughed. "Honey, what do you think I dream about when I'm in bed?" she quipped. "And, this is with him sleeping in the same house as me. I know I don't have a shot at him because he thinks of me like his sister. But you, on the other hand, appear to have the inside track of what every woman in southern Saskatchewan could only dream about. You've been given a Golden Ticket, Amanda. Don't waste the opportunity."

The two women continued to chat for a while longer. Ashley promised to keep it quiet from Kevin and Cecil because they knew if the guys found out it would become common knowledge all over Melville by sunset. It was the type of town where everybody knew who everyone was, and the smallest bit of gossip would turn a secret into a front page story in the local newspaper, the Melville Advance. It would be the type of attention a person like Hank would want to shy away from, and could drive him out of town. It would be a huge loss to the farm, and neither Amanda, nor Ashley wanted that to happen.

After reassuring one another they would do their best to keep it amongst themselves, the girls decided to call it a night. Amanda headed off to bed more conflicted than she was before. Was Hank showing an interest in her? She tried to fall asleep, but her mind was racing with the thought of what could be. It was a dream she did not want to wake from.

CHAPTER EIGHT

The dawn came early, and Amanda awoke restless. She had been unable to sleep because her mind was racing with the thoughts of the night before. She knew she could not go downstairs for breakfast looking the way she did. It would be something that would draw the inquisitive ire of the boys, and could lead to her secret getting out. Amanda rushed to her bathroom and took a cleansing shower in a bid to wake herself up. After pruning her hair and applying a layer of make-up to make her look less disheveled, Amanda threw on her clothes, and made her way downstairs to meet the others for breakfast.

Cecil was pouring himself a glass of orange juice when he saw her. "'Morning, Amanda," he greeted.

"Good morning, everyone," the heir said. "Would you mind pouring a glass for me please, Cecil?"

Cecil grabbed the empty glass in front of her spot at the table, and filled it. "Sure thing," he replied, "anything to help the boss out."

Amanda accepted the beverage. "Thank you," she said. "What time did you guys get in last night from the bar?"

Kevin appeared from the kitchen with a plate of sausage links. He replied, "I'd say it was around 11. We could have stayed longer, but Ashley talked us into heading back here early."

Ashley yelled from the kitchen, "I wanted to make sure you guys still had part of your livers in advance of Friday night. Besides, there are still some things that need to be done around the farm, and you two aren't going to be any help if you're both hung over."

72

"Yes, mother," Kevin mocked.

Ashley asked, "I'm frying up some eggs for us, Amanda. How do you like yours?"

"I'll have a couple over easy please, Ashley," she said. "I should limit myself because of the whole cholesterol concerns about them."

Ashley laughed. "If the cholesterol doesn't kill you," she said, "the grease from frying this stuff should. But, I made sure to pat the sausages dry after they came out of the pan."

Hank entered the dining room, and a smile emerged on Amanda's face; her mind filled with memories from the night before. Hank was dressed in black denim jeans and a blue plaid shirt. His blond hair was coiffed with a bit of a spike, and his blue eyes were subdued compared to the night before.

"Good morning, everyone," he greeted. "Amanda, you look nice today."

Amanda scoffed at the thought. If only Hank knew about the sleepless night the heir had because of the confused feelings she experienced after their kiss. Amanda attempted to downplay things and said, "Thank you, Hank, and might I say you look dapper this morning, as well."

Kevin and Cecil looked at each other, and murmured, "What the hell is going on?" But, before they could pry further, Ashley came in from the kitchen with everyone's eggs. As she set their plates in front of them, Ashley gave the boys the evil eye; warning not to ask any questions if they knew what was good for them. "I have to concur with both of you," Ashley commented, "the two of you *do* look gorgeous this morning."

Hank said, "Thank you, Ashley. I hope these two didn't keep you up all night with their carousing."

"It was nothing a crack of the whip couldn't control," she said. "It was like I was saying earlier; I had to make sure the boys paced themselves ahead of next Friday night. If they got disorderly, we'd have to relocate our little outing to Yorkton or elsewhere, and I'd prefer to keep it local."

Amanda agreed, "Same here; if any of us do have a few too many, I'd hate for us to have to drive any great distance to get back here. The last thing I want is for us to pull over to the side of the highway because one of us couldn't hold their liquor."

Cecil argued, "Yorkton's not that far from here. It's only 25 miles to the northeast."

"That's 20 miles too far for my liking," the heir said, "and I'm sure the RCMP wouldn't appreciate it if we were pulled over on the side of Highway 10 because you had to puke your guts out."

Kevin chuffed, "Me thinks you've been hanging around Ashley for too long. She's starting to rub off on you."

Ashley and Amanda stared daggers at him. "Excuse *us*?!?" Ashley exclaimed. "I'm rubbing off on her? Let me tell you something, buddy…"

Hank stood up, and attempted to defuse the situation. "Everybody, please settle down," he begged. "I know everyone is on edge because of what could transpire on Gerald's night, but we're losing sight of the real reason why we're going out to begin with. We're doing it to honour Gerald, and by fighting about it, or conducting ourselves in a disorderly manner is being disrespectful to him. Gerald meant a lot to us, and to the people in this community. I think we all owe it to Gerald to give him the dignity and respect he deserves."

Ashley calmed down and replied, "You're right, Hank. We shouldn't be arguing about something so petty. Gerald was a great man; he's done so much to bring us together, and made us the family we are today. In turn, he's brought Amanda into our lives, and has given us the extension of him we've been missing since his untimely passing. Kevin, Cecil, I'm sorry for accusing you both of not behaving appropriately."

Kevin sighed. "To be honest," he said, "I should be the one apologizing. I can understand where you're coming from. We're representatives of Gerald, and while we were looking out for our own personal interests, we've lost sight of why we are here in the first place. We should hold Gerald's memory in a higher regard, not tarnish the legacy he's left behind."

Cecil chimed in, "I'm with Kevin on this. We wanted to celebrate a job well done with this year's planting, but we've forgotten we've recently lost our father figure. We should take the time to honour his memory, and remember the great times we've all had with him. Before Gerald, we were individuals living our own lives. Thanks to him, we've all bonded and became the family we are today. One week from tonight, we shall raise our glasses, and toast the great man who has touched us all."

Everyone nodded in agreement. Amanda looked on, and ran her finger along the rim of her juice glass. She was daydreaming about Hank again. This time, she thought about how he would make a wonderful father after observing how he was able to defuse the situation between Kevin and Ashley. It was firm, but he did not raise his voice at either of them. It was a type of disciplinary style that appealed to her, and made her wonder what life would be like with him by her side, as they raised their future children together. Amanda's daze was broken when Ashley nudged the plate of sausages against the dreamer's check.

"Wakey-wakey, Shake 'n Bakey," Ashley threatened. "If you don't give me an answer, I'm dumping a couple of links into your orange juice."

"I'm sorry, Ashley. Was I daydreaming again?"

Cecil noted, "Yes, you were. What's gotten into you? I've never seen anyone ignore an offer of sausages cooked by Ashley before."

Kevin asked, "You've been in a haze at the breakfast table quite often lately. Is there something on your mind that's been troubling you?"

Amanda was at a loss for words. She looked towards Hank, who was looking straight at her. Should she let the cat out of the bag, and face the inevitable music? Hank didn't say a word, but gave a flirtatious wink at her.

Ashley rushed in and made the save. "Can't a girl be alone with her thoughts?" she accused. "Honestly, you two are worse than a public inquiry into Senate spending."

Kevin reasoned, "We're just concerned about her, that's all."

Amanda replied, "I appreciate the fact you guys are worried about me, but I'm fine, really. I'm just trying to get used to everything that's been going on between the farm, family, and work back in Toronto. I've been trying to juggle it all, and it's been overwhelming at times."

"It is quite an adjustment," Hank noted. "But, you know we're all here to support you, and each other as we adjust to everything that's gone on."

Ashley added, "You'll probably feel better when we all go out together on Friday night to remember your uncle. We'll sit, relax, have a drink or two, and remember what a great man he was."

"I'm sure you're right," Amanda said. "I need to slow down, and appreciate the opportunity I've been given: to run the family business, and meet the wonderful people I have, so far."

"Speaking of which," Kevin asked, "how are you coming along on that financial assistance request?"

"I plan on going into town today to see if I can get some progress done," she replied. "In the meantime, I'm looking into getting a short-term loan to help make ends meet."

Cecil inquired, "That would be great if you could. I hope you don't have to put up anything big for collateral."

Ashley chimed in, "I'm sure Amanda can negotiate something that doesn't put our operations in jeopardy." Then, she winked at her supervisor.

Amanda was confused. Why would Ashley make such a gesture? Did the female staffer know something she didn't? Amanda was going to quiz her employee until the heir's gaze met Hank's again. He smiled at her with his blue eyes. Amanda had no other choice, but to smile back. However, she shifted her eyes to look at everyone else, so the others wouldn't catch on. Diverting the conversation away from what was going on in her mind, she asked, "So, what's on tap for everyone today?"

Ashley replied, "Well, with the fields seeded, I'm hoping the boys will help me in the barn to get the processor up and running. I know it's early, but I don't want any delays when it comes time to harvest a few months from now."

Kevin and Cecil protested, but they knew she was right. They weren't much of a help when they were out in the fields. Now, they had no excuse not to give Ashley a hand.

"What about you, Amanda?" Hank inquired. "What's on today's agenda for you?"

"I got a call from Linda yesterday to come over to her place for a visit. Little Nate has been missing his cousin since I moved in here, so I'm going to stop by for a spell before I head to the Ministry branch office in Yorkton."

Cecil was confused. "Wait a minute," he asked, "you weren't over there last night? I thought I heard you tell Ashley that you were going out after dinner."

Kevin added, "Now that you mention it, I remember hearing that, too. So, if you weren't at your sister-in-law's, where did you go?"

Amanda gulped hard over the discovery of the hole in her story. Amanda was in a bind; she couldn't tell Kevin and Cecil she was out having coffee with Hank the night before. Amanda would never hear the end of it, and the whole town would know within a matter of hours. Should she continue to lie to her new family, or should she come clean about what really happened? Everyone looked towards the head of the table with concern. Amanda closed her eyes, took a deep breath, and made her confession.

"If you must know," Amanda announced, "I was out on a date last night."

78

The dining room went silent, save for the cutlery hitting everyone's plates in shock.

CHAPTER NINE

Cecil was the first one to speak. "You went out with someone?" he asked.

Amanda nodded. "I was," she said.

Kevin spoke up next. "Who was the lucky guy?"

"I don't believe the two of you would know my date," Amanda replied. "Leonard introduced me to him while I was staying at my cousin's before I moved into here. We've kept in touch since then, and we met up for coffee last night."

Ashley leaned in and whispered, "Smooth half-truth; letting them know you were on a coffee date, but not telling them it was with 'you know who.'"

Hank decided to play along with the others. "So, when are we going to meet this mystery man? You know you're going to have to bring him around to meet us."

Amanda glared at the journeyman. She couldn't believe Hank was going to make her sweat over the lie; however, Amanda was relieved he was being a good sport about it. "I guess I *could* ask if he's free next Friday night, and see if he'd like to join us," she said.

Ashley commented, "It couldn't hurt. We have to make sure we approve of this guy. Gerald wouldn't have it any less."

Kevin quipped, "Listen to the Farm Mom, Amanda. She knows what's good for all of us around here." Ashley retaliated by throwing a sausage link at him.

Cecil attempted to restore order. He stated, "All kidding aside, as weird as this may sound, you're a part of our family, and we want to make sure this guy – whoever he is – is the type of person who will treat you right. You know we're looking out for your best interests."

The sentiment touched Amanda. To be considered a family member instead of just their boss showed a level of acceptance she didn't expect. "I know," she said, "and I appreciate the fact all of you care enough to make sure I don't get hurt. I'll give him a call after breakfast."

"Does that mean we can listen in on the conversation?" Kevin teased.

Amanda smirked, "On second thought, I'll call him from Linda's. The last thing I need is to have some 'nosy kids' eavesdropping on their adopted sister's phone calls."

Ashley laughed. "That'll learn ya," she crowed. "You lot are like a bunch of kids. I swear; the next thing you know, Kevin will be trying to float Cecil's shoes down Pearl Creek."

"Well, boys will be boys," Amanda said. "But, I do appreciate the good-natured ribbing. I never had any brothers of my own, so Kevin and Cecil make up for it; although, a little more maturity would be appreciated."

Cecil turned to Kevin and said, "I guess that means we're going to have to cancel the plans to put a toad in her shoes."

Amanda rolled her eyes. "Honestly, I don't know about you two," she said.

Hank chuckled and added, "Knowing these two, it might be a good idea that you didn't."

"Et tu, Hank," Kevin accused. "I thought you had our backs here."

"Sorry guys, but knowing how much clout the girls have, I'm going to know my place and side with them."

"Thank you, Hank," Ashley said before commenting to Kevin and Cecil, "you two could learn a lot from him."

Breakfast continued on with some more light hearted ribbing. Once the meal was over, Amanda and Ashley cleared the table and began to wash the dishes. The guys headed out to the barn, but while the heir was washing the dishes, she found herself in a daydream.

~ * * * ~

Hank would make his way to the kitchen where the women were in the middle of scrubbing the frying pans.

"Ashley," he stated, "I sent the guys into the barn, but I don't really trust them to be alone in there."

"Couldn't you keep an eye on them?" Ashley asked. "We're in the middle of doing the dishes."

"I'll finish in here for you," he said. "Besides, I'd like to speak with Amanda for a bit."

The women exchanged glances with one another. Both of them knew what he wanted to talk about. Ashley set down her dish cloth and replied, "I better get in there before those two end up wrecking something; have fun, you two." She scurried off, and closed the front door behind her.

Hank grabbed the discarded cloth and joined in. He said, "That was an interesting white lie you told in there earlier."

"I'm sorry," Amanda replied. "I had to say something to get them off my back. Those two seem to be like a couple of bloodhounds; trying to sniff out any bit of incriminating evidence."

"No, no, it was quite commendable. You were meeting someone out for coffee last night, but gave them the impression it was this mysterious stranger who had swept you off your feet."

"Would it be a lie if I said the man I did meet with last night had done so?"

"He must have been quite a guy if he was able to do it over a cup of coffee."

"I must admit, he was quite a charmer. I'm just surprised with all of the women he could choose from in town, he opted for a complex gal like me."

Hank moved behind Amanda, and wrapped his arms around her waist. "Maybe he saw something in you those other women didn't have."

She turned around and faced him. "And, what might that be, exactly?" she asked.

"A wonderful woman with a great personality, a radiance that could light up a room, and I must confess, the softest, most kissable lips around."

Taking her cue, Amanda placed her hands on the sides of Hank's face, and raised herself up to kiss him. His lips had a greasy aftertaste from their breakfast, but she didn't mind it at all. Hank gathered Amanda into his arms, and sat her down on the edge of the counter with care. He moved in towards her, and continued their romantic embrace. Amanda's mouth hungrily searched for his, as she started to tug the back of his shirt upwards; her nails scratching the small of his back. He winced at her aggressiveness, but continued to kiss her with a hunger.

Amanda broke away, and started unbuttoning Hank's shirt. Her breathing was becoming more frantic. She wanted to get him naked as quickly as possible, but knew she had to be patient. "One article at a time," she thought. Amanda leaned forward and started nibbling on his bottom lip. Hank's hands slipped underneath the back of her blouse, and caressed her tender flesh. This brought a sigh from her lips. Amanda didn't want the moment to end.

Once she unfastened the last button, Amanda pushed Hank's shirt off of his shoulders. The heat radiated off of his muscular chest. She ran her hands along the newly exposed skin, and felt how developed his pectoral muscles were. All of the years Hank had spent as a labourer paid off; it was the equivalent of spending countless of hours in a gym. This drove Amanda deeper into lust for him. She leaned forward and kissed him with ferocious passion. He had no other choice, but to reciprocate.

Amanda tilted her head slightly; inviting Hank to start kissing the side of her neck. He didn't disappoint, as he lowered his mouth to offer his felicitations. The attention he was giving her was starting to arouse Amanda. She had not been with a man for years. Now, Hank was getting her engine purring. But, if it was a low hum before, it shifted into another gear when Hank removed his hand from the small of Amanda's back to cup one of her breasts. Another moan escaped from her lips, and she knew she had to have him. "Let the others working in the barn be damned," she thought.

Amanda trailed her hands down Hank's bare chest, and toyed with his belt buckle before she trailed her fingers over the front of his jeans. Her eyes grew in astonishment, as she felt his arousal strain against the denim. She had to set him free. Hank, unbeknownst to Amanda's intentions, pressed against her, and noticed a slight dampness emanating from the crotch of her pants. Realizing what was about to transpire, Hank broke away from their embrace.

"I'm sorry, Amanda," he apologized. "This is going faster than I intended it to."

"What's the problem?" she asked. "It looked like you were getting into it as much as I was."

"I was, but I think it's too early for us to take that step."

"Excuse me, but if I recall correctly, you're the one who came up behind me and wrapped your arms around my waist."

"I did, and I thought all we were going to do was share a kiss and an embrace. But, things escalated far beyond that."

Amanda pouted like a spoiled child who was denied a desired toy.

"Please, don't give me that look," he begged. "I like you, Amanda, and I think you are a wonderful woman. Heck, I wouldn't mind starting a relationship with you."

Amanda's jaw dropped in astonishment. "You... you want to start a relationship... with me?" she asked.

"Yes, I do, but I want things between us to develop naturally. I don't want us to ruin that with a frenzied romp in the sack."

Amanda sighed, "I guess you're right. You did say you didn't care for women who were only after you for your body."

"Yes, and I'm afraid we were on that same road I'm reluctant to travel on. I hope you can understand where I'm coming from."

"It's unfair that you got me going the way you did."

"I know, and I apologize for that. But in fairness, you got me rather hot and bothered, too."

A smile crept on Amanda's face. "I guess we'll have to take a rain check for our erotic behaviour," she suggested.

"We will, and I promise I will make it up to you. But, I want us to take things slow, and build up to it. Personally, I feel it would be worth the wait."

"I'm going to hold you to that, Hank Acker."

Hank grabbed his shirt off the floor, and started to re-button it. "I better get to the barn before the others start wondering where I ran off to."

Amanda resigned herself. "Yes, we can't have our cover blown."

"Do you think you can pass me that damp dish cloth? I want to get rid of any evidence."

Amanda threw the rag at Hank; smacking him in the face. He noted, "You must really be upset; you fired that at me."

"What do you expect? You got me all wound up, and left me hanging. You're nothing but a tease."

"Rest assured, Amanda. I may be a tease, but in due time, I *will* please." Hank finished wiping his face, and leaned in to give her a quick kiss on the lips.

"Run along now; the others are waiting."

Hank rushed out the door, and headed for the barn; the door slamming behind him. Amanda eased herself off the counter, and let out an exasperated sigh. She was denied her wish this time around, but with Hank's promise, Amanda knew one day, it would come true.

~ * * * ~

Amanda snapped back to reality when she was splashed by her female employee.

"Quit sticking your head in the clouds, boss lady," Ashley ordered. "The dishes aren't going to rinse and dry themselves, you know."

"I'm sorry," Amanda apologized. "I must've gone into a daydream."

Ashley smirked. "Why do I have a feeling it's over a certain man in the barn?" she said.

"I know I shouldn't," the heir resigned, "but I can't get Hank out of my head."

Ashley patted Amanda's hand. "Look, honey," she said, "you have to keep in mind that while he's got a pretty face, and a hot body to match, he is still your employee."

"I am aware of that, Ashley," Amanda said. "However, the daydream I just had made me think about a lot more than him working for me."

The heir would recount the dream to her employee. Ashley was shocked to hear about the erotic details of their imagined 'near-coitus', but hung on every word. After Amanda finished telling her fantasy, Ashley attempted to advise her supervisor.

"That's quite a dilemma you're in," Ashley stated.

"You're telling me," Amanda said. "I know it's wrong to have such feelings and desires for Hank, but there's something in the back of my head that's telling me we're meant to be together. It's as if Uncle Gerald's hand is guiding me towards him."

"Amanda," Ashley scolded, "Gerald might be bringing you and Hank together in some fashion, but I highly doubt sex is what he had in mind at this time."

"I know he didn't," the heir said, "but there's something within me that wants there to be."

Ashley sighed. "Look, honey," she said, "your hormones have obviously shifted into overdrive after your 'coffee date' last night. You need to step back, and seriously re-evaluate the situation. Hank might or might not be your soul mate, I don't know; however, for the time being he is still your employee, and you cannot ignore that."

Amanda resigned herself. "You're right," she said. "I don't want there to be any ill will between the two of us should I pursue him further and it's not welcomed. I have to be rational, and not give into my primal urges."

Ashley patted her supervisor on the back. "Perhaps talking to Linda will give you a little more clarity on this matter," she said. "It might help to get a different perspective on the situation."

"Thanks, Ashley," Amanda said. "I appreciate the suggestion."

The two women would finish the dishes, and after they were put away, Amanda left for her cousin's, with the hopes of getting her head and heart straightened out.

CHAPTER TEN

Amanda pulled up to the modest home, and gave herself a quick once over in her rear-view mirror. She would hate to have look dishevelled from the thoughts that ran through her head earlier. The ad executive got out of her car, and saw an exuberant child rush towards her. "Cousin Amanda's here!" Nathan shouted with glee.

Amanda knelt down and scooped the young boy into her arms. "How's my favourite little man doing?" she asked. "Have you been behaving yourself?"

He replied, "I have, but Stripes is hiding from me."

"Oh," she said. "If he's hiding from you, you must have done something to scare him off."

"He's probably sleeping somewhere upstairs," Nathan reasoned.

"Then, you should let him sleep," Amanda replied. "Don't worry; he'll come around when he wakes up."

Nathan smiled. "Okay then," he said.

Linda came out of the house to join the pair. "Good morning, Amanda," she said. "So glad you could make it out today."

"I know, I'm sorry," Amanda apologized. "Things have been hectic around the farm, and I haven't had a chance to get away until last night."

Linda recognized, "Ah yes, last night. Here, let me take Nate from you. It's almost time for his nap, and we can talk about it in private."

Amanda handed Nathan off to his mother and replied, "I'd appreciate that because a lot has happened in the past 24 hours."

"Oh, sounds juicy. I can't wait to find out about it."

~ * * * ~

Linda put her son down for his snooze; then, went into the kitchen to put the coffee on for herself and her guest. Once it had brewed, she poured a couple of mugs, and joined Amanda at the kitchen table.

Linda stated, "The last time we talked it was before your coffee date with Hank. I'm guessing things went well between the two of you."

"It did," Amanda said. "We found out a lot about each other; our respective pasts, our interests, and the type of things we look for in a prospective mate."

"That must have made for an interesting conversation," Linda said. "I hope you weren't too distracted with his rugged good looks."

Amanda confessed, "I must admit, it was a challenge. But, I felt comfortable sitting in the Timmy's and having a conversation with him. He has a calming personality about him, and when the dim light of the store made his eyes sparkle, I had to do my best not to melt into them right there and then."

"I bet they are lovely to look at," Linda mused.

Amanda said, "They were just one part of the total package: his eyes, his voice, his smile. If you based him on just those three things, he's swoon-worthy. But, when you throw in everything else he's got going on below the neck, it makes him even more desirable."

Linda nodded. "He certainly is easy on the eyes," she said, "I won't deny that."

Amanda continued, "And, to top it all off, he is a perfect gentleman. He's not one of these guys who buys into his own hype, and beds every woman who throws themselves at him. He prefers to stick to one woman and one woman only."

"Well," Linda said, "whoever is lucky enough to corral that steer will be the envy of every woman from the Rockies to Lake of The Woods."

Amanda took a deep breath. "If the scenario that's been playing out in my head comes true," she said, "I might have to prepare myself to be the most hated woman in all of Western Canada."

Linda blinked, "Does that mean what I think it means?"

"If you think it means I'm wishing for Hank to develop an interest in me; then, yes."

"Welcome to the club, Amanda," Linda replied. "Every woman who has come into contact with him has wanted to be involved with him in some capacity. Mind you, from what I hear, most of it has been in a sexual nature."

Amanda blushed at her cousin's statement, knowing of the daydream she had a mere hour earlier. "I know it's wrong to be

thinking about a relationship with someone who works for me,"
she said. "There are all the ramifications where I could be charged
for sexual harassment should I make a play for Hank and it's not
accepted. It's just... part of me can see the two of us together as a
couple."

"Hmm, then if you plan on making your move, you need to do so
by next Sunday."

It didn't sink in with Amanda at first, but it began to dawn on her.
She was due to fly back to Toronto to resume her advertising
executive duties full-time then. Amanda knew if she was going to
win Hank's heart, she would need to do so soon. And even if she
were successful in snagging the journeyman before she left, would
Hank stay faithful to her when she wasn't around? The women of
Melville would do their best to lead him astray, and attempt to
convince Hank it would be better to be involved with a local
woman instead of someone over 1500 miles away. Amanda was
scared of such a possibility. Hank was everything she could ask for
in a companion. However, the notion she could win Hank, and
then lose him when she left Saskatchewan worried her.

Amanda sighed, "I've heard about the challenges long-distance
relationships face. There are trust and loyalty issues between both
people involved. In the event he were to become mine, I wish there
was some way I could be sure Hank would remain true to me after
I've left town."

"Has he given you any indication his interest might waver," Linda
asked. "For example, has his head turned away to look at another
woman while you were talking to him?"

"No," Amanda said. "Whenever the two of us have talked, his
attention has always been on me. He is respectful in that sense. It's
just the notion of him here, and I'm back in Toronto, I don't know

92

if he could fend off all of the women around town, and still maintain his focus on me."

"Well," Linda said, "as the saying goes, 'Absence makes the heart go fonder.' Perhaps the two of you would fall deeper for one another when there is such a huge distance between the two of you."

"I hope you're right, Linda," Amanda said. "It would be a shame if he were to leave me for someone else. After the daydream I had before coming over, I couldn't begin to imagine my life without him."

Linda did a double-take. "Whoa, whoa, back up for a second there. What are you talking about?"

Amanda told her cousin about the dream she had in the kitchen after that morning's breakfast: the embrace, the passionate kissing, and the arousal she and Hank both experienced. Amanda was getting flustered recounting the events. Then, showed her disappointment when she described how he backed away; citing the fact he believed things were progressing too fast for his liking. Linda comforted Amanda over the imagined rejection, but assured her it was her perception of Hank respecting her, and didn't want to jeopardize a relationship she wanted the two of them to build. Linda's words soothed Amanda's soul, and gave her some confidence. Amanda trusted Hank's judgment, but this was but a mere fantasy. She didn't know how he would react if and when she would ask him to change their relationship from employer-employee to a more romantic one. Amanda decided she would continue to play things cool for now, but would plan for her next move in case the opportunity presented itself.

"So, Ashley knows about this little daydream, then?" Linda asked.

"She does," Amanda said. "Naturally, she was shocked to hear it, and she's still cautioning me about the whole 'he works for you' factoid. I told her I can't help it, but I can honestly see myself as Hank's significant other. I'm hoping she will keep it between her and me. I'd hate for this to get back to the guys; especially, Kevin and Cecil."

"I'm sure Ashley will keep it under her hat," Linda reasoned. "Hank finding out would be embarrassing enough as it is, but Kevin and Cecil knowing that you're warm for Hank's form? They would have it all over town in no time flat, and you'd have a bigger situation on your hands than you wished for."

"That's something I can't let happen," Amanda said. "I haven't seen Hank get angry before, but I'm sure if the right buttons are pressed, he would make short work of anyone who got on his bad side."

The two women continued to chat about what else had been going on over the previous few days. Leonard was still keeping his ear to the ground about any legal actions Rebecca might attempt to wrest the farm away from Amanda, but he had not heard anything yet from Mr. Mitchell. Whatever Rebecca was plotting, she was keeping her cards close to her chest. It was a notion which worried Amanda, but one she would have to deal with if and when the time came.

After spending a couple of hours talking, Amanda started to get ready to head back to the farm.

"Do you have to leave so soon?" Linda asked.

"I'd like to stay longer," Amanda replied, "but, I have to start getting dinner ready. Plus, I want to try to see if I could have a word with Hank beforehand."

Linda blinked. "Are you sure that's wise after your fantasized wet and wild foreplay at the sink?" she asked.

"Linda," Amanda said, "it's like the saying goes, 'If you can't stand the heat; then, get out of the kitchen.' I'm just hoping any 'hotness' I experience is subdued, in case anyone should pick up on my vibes."

Linda laughed. "I hope if anyone does, it's Ashley. She seems to be the most mature out of the rest of them."

Amanda nodded. "Agreed," she said. "Kevin and Cecil would probably hoot, holler, and catcall at the idea of my wanting to get it on with Hank."

"But, you have to be careful about Ashley, too. She might be so envious of your fantasy she'd want to join in."

Amanda gagged at the thought. "As much of a nice gal Ashley is," she replied, "I don't share my fantasies. She's going to have to find her own hunk-and-a-half to dream about."

Amanda kissed a waking Nathan on his forehead, and gave Linda a hug goodbye. She asked if Linda and Leonard were going to make it out for drinks the following Friday night. Her cousin said they would try their best to make it out; it would depend on being able to find a sitter for Nathan. Amanda left her cousin's house and drove towards Yorkton, in hopes she could cross the other item on her "To do" list before heading back to the farm.

~ * * * ~

Amanda arrived at the Saskatchewan Ministry of Agriculture branch in Yorkton an hour after leaving Linda's. The heir took a number, and awaited her turn. She caught a bit of a break when she saw the line-up to speak to a representative wasn't very long; only ten people were ahead of her. Once her number was called, she approached the service desk. Amanda explained the situation to the clerk, and filled out some necessary claim forms. She was dismayed over the fact she had to pay a processing fee, but as with most government services, if there was a way to bilk the taxpayer for it, they would. It was something she had learned the hard way after spending the previous five years in Ontario.

Amanda paid the fee, and asked the clerk, "How long will it be until I learn if I've been approved? The farm really needs the assistance as soon as possible."

"The standard processing time is three-to-four weeks," the clerk said.

Amanda was shocked. "Three-to-four weeks?!?" she exclaimed. "I don't know if my farm can survive for that long. Is there any way you can expedite the claim?"

"Ms. Bellamy," the clerk explained, "I understand of your plight, but unfortunately, there is a review process that your claim has to go through. It's not just your claim, but everyone who files one has the same waiting period. We have to make sure no one is submitting a bogus claim in a bid to defraud the province."

Amanda nodded, and thanked the clerk for his help. The heir walked back to her car, climbed into the driver's seat, and buried her face in her hands. She didn't know how to break the news to the others, but silently prayed for whomever Hank was going to ask for a loan would come through.

CHAPTER ELEVEN

When Amanda returned to the farm, everyone was finishing up their lunch in the dining room. She failed to realize how long she had spent not only at Linda's house, but at the ministry office in Yorkton. Because of it, she was feeling some hunger pains. She attempted to sneak past the others, but it proved to be all for not.

"Welcome back, Amanda," Kevin greeted. "Did you have a nice visit over at Linda's?"

"Oh yes," she answered. "We sat and talked for a couple of hours over coffee."

Ashley probed, "How is she doing?"

"She's doing well," Amanda replied, "and little Nate was happy to see me. He didn't get to spend much time with me, as Linda was just about to put him down for his nap when I got there, and he didn't wake up until I was leaving."

"That must have been disappointing for him," Cecil commented. "He was so excited to see you again, and then when you got there, he was shuttled off to bed."

"It was," Amanda said, "but, I hope to make it up to him again later this week. It's not often he gets a chance to see me since we're at different ends of the country, so I want to try to spend as much time as I can with him."

"Did you have any luck at the Ministry office in Yorkton?" Kevin asked.

The look on Amanda's face was filled with sadness. "I filed a claim in hopes they can provide some financial assistance," she

97

said. "However, they said it's going to take about three-to-four weeks to process and investigate it. I tried to get them to speed the process up, so we could get the assistance quicker, but they weren't ready to give us any preferential treatment. I'm sorry, everyone. I did the best I could."

The mood at the dining room table turned into a solemn one. Cecil was the first to break the silence.

"Damn the bureaucratic red tape," he cursed. "You'd think with an industry as important as ours, they'd be quicker in going through all of the claims."

"I'm not a fan of it either," Amanda said, "but I understand this is the procedure they go through. We just have to scrape by until the hand down their ruling."

"Things are tight enough as they are," Kevin complained. "How are we going to keep this place running until then, and this still hinges on the hope we are approved. What's going to happen if we're turned down? We'll all be royally fucked then."

Amanda looked at Hank, and non-verbally asked him if she should tell them about his plan. Hank didn't say a word, but nodded in her direction. She closed her eyes, let out a deep breath, and said to everyone, "I'm working on finding someone who could help us out in the short term."

"Are you asking Leonard and Linda to help us out?" Ashley asked.

"Actually," Hank interrupted, "I'm the one who's going to be looking into finding someone who can bail us out."

"Really," Cecil said, "who do you have in mind?"

"I can't really say," Hank said, "but I have a good feeling they'll be able to come through for us." He then winked at Ashley, who nodded back at him.

"Couldn't you give us a little hint?" Kevin pressed.

"Mind your own business," Ashley scolded her co-worker. "I'm sure whoever Hank has lined up would prefer to remain a private investor. We should be thankful anyone is willing to offer to help us in the first place."

Amanda breathed easier after Hank's assurance there would be some money coming the farm's way; however, she, too, was curious as to the identity of the proposed mystery investor. Regardless, she trusted Hank's judgment, and began to see him a little more as an equal than as an employee. "But, enough about this investor," she said. "How is the work in the barn coming along?"

Hank replied, "We're getting a good amount done today. Ashley's making sure we remain focused on the task at hand, and that certain others aren't goofing off."

"What's with all the hate, Hank?" Cecil asked. "We're efficient workers."

"You are," Ashley interjected, "but, you two have to be supervised to make sure it gets done. You'd get your work done a lot sooner if you weren't distracted by every prairie dog that pops its head out of the ground."

Kevin defended, "We can't help it; we're amused by their ADHD behaviour."

Ashley chuffed, "If you ask me, it sounds more like you two are the ones who have ADHD."

"Easy there, Ashley," Amanda interrupted. "We don't need this to escalate into another argument like the one we had this morning."

"You're right, Amanda," Ashley said. "Sorry about that, guys."

Kevin said, "That's alright. We accept the criticism, but you know we do the best we can."

"I know you do, and I appreciate it," Ashley said. "It's just there's a time and a place for everything, and the way I see it: the faster we get the necessary things done, the more time we have to rest and enjoy the fruits of our labour."

Cecil corrected, "Um, I thought we grew corn. So technically, shouldn't that be the *grains* of our labour?"

Ashley rolled her eyes. "Semantics," she stated, "but, as long as you got the gist of what I meant."

Hank chuckled at the banter between his co-workers. Amanda noticed he was glancing in her direction. He gave her an apologetic look; one that said, "I hope you don't mind me confessing about the fact I'm working behind the scenes in getting the farm some funding, but I did it to calm the others' fears." She smiled back at Hank and nodded; letting him know that everything was alright. Her eyes conveyed an additional message, "I hope we could have some time to further talk, alone." Hank didn't say a word, but nodded in acknowledgement.

Amanda snapped from her silent conversation when Ashley asked, "Weren't you on your way to the kitchen to grab something?"

"Yes, I was," Amanda said. "I didn't know what we had left in the line of cold meat for sandwiches."

"I think there's still some cooked ham left in the fridge," Kevin replied. "There should be some cheese slices in there, too."

Ashley got up from the table and offered, "I'll help you find them."

Cecil turned to the others and commented, "Those two are having a lot of one-on-one conversations lately."

Hank mused, "They must be talking about that guy Amanda went out with last night. You know how women like to gossip."

Amanda called out from the kitchen, "We can still hear you, guys. You'd think you were as bad as us."

The men laughed at the accusation, but in actual fact, they were.

~ * * * ~

Ashley made her way over to the fridge and retrieved the food items from it, while Amanda grabbed herself a plate.

Ashley said, "We haven't spoken since this morning since you left for Linda's. I'm sorry to hear things didn't go as well as you hoped in Yorkton."

"I am, too," Amanda said. "I was hoping there would be a positive result when I spoke to a representative."

"Well," Ashley said, "at least Hank's finding someone who'll back us until the Ministry comes back with their ruling."

"That's if the Ministry decides in our favour and cuts us a cheque," Amanda stated. "They might not be that generous since we have this year's crop in the ground already."

"We'll cross that bridge when we come to it," Ashley said. "In the meantime, we have to make sure Hank can work his magic and convince the investor – whoever it is – to bail us out in our time of need."

Amanda didn't want to doubt the journeyman's campaigning, but she wondered how someone who had only worked blue collar jobs would be able to convince someone to dole out an adequate amount of cash to keep a small business, like a corn farm, afloat. She was the one who had the expertise in marketing. She ought to be the one to make the pitch. However, Hank was more well-known to the people in the area. She was reluctant, but for once, she had to trust someone else's judgment.

"Hank must think we're a special group if he's willing to find someone to help us out," Ashley mused.

"It's a thoughtful and touching gesture on his part," Amanda said. "It shows he respects Uncle Gerald's legacy, and cares about the farm enough to do whatever it takes to keep the place alive. It's casting a whole new light upon him, and I'm starting to respect him on a whole new level."

Ashley concluded, "Hank really is one of a kind, isn't he?"

"He certainly is," Amanda said, "and I am very fortunate to know him, and consider him not only a co-worker, but a good friend, as well."

"Does this mean you're giving up your ambition of pursuing a relationship with him?" Ashley asked. "Because if you still are, you only have a little more than one week to capture his heart before you leave to head back to Toronto."

"Not in the slightest," Amanda said. "I'd be lying if I said my upcoming departure wasn't something that concerned me. If I was successful, I'm not sure how he would react to the prospect of a long-distance relationship. Shit, I'm not even sure how *I* would react. Would the two of us stay committed to each other through the miles apart?"

Ashley patted the heir's hand. "Amanda, sweetie, I can't answer that from your perspective; only you know how you're going to feel if and when the time comes. As for Hank, I can't say for him either, but I will do my best to make sure he doesn't forget should things end up going down that road for you both."

Amanda smiled. "Thank you, I appreciate that."

"What are pseudo-sisters for? Besides, I know how much he means to you. I can't say whether or not that feeling is mutual, but from what I can tell, he must think you're someone special if he's willing to go out to coffee with you, and not bemoan about you ogling him. The way I see it, if the two of you are destined to be together, you will be. Fate is what is bringing the two of you together originally, and the mutual respect is what will keep you together; whether it's as good friends, or something more."

Amanda finished preparing her sandwich, and the women returned to the dining room where the guys; who were trying to listen in on their conversation attempted to act casual. Both Ashley and Amanda exchanged glances with each other; then, smirked at them.

"You're not going to fool us, boys," Ashley stated. "We know you two were trying to eavesdrop on us."

"Can you blame us?" Cecil defended. "The conversations you two have are more interesting than anything the three of us could come up with."

"Yeah, right," Amanda chuffed. "You three are just being nosy."

Kevin reasoned, "We're just a couple of concerned brothers, that's all. We don't want to see you get hurt."

"I appreciate that, but I'm a big girl. I can handle myself. Besides, if this guy you all are concerned about screws me over, I have no problem placing my knee in his crotch."

Hank winced at the mental image, but did it in a jovial sense where he felt empathetic to the mystery man's pain. "I wouldn't want to be in his shoes if that happened," he replied.

Amanda ate a bite of her sandwich and smiled, "Well, as long as he's a good boy, and treats me right, then he won't have to feel my wrath. Like the saying goes, 'Hell hath no fury like a woman scorned'."

CHAPTER TWELVE

The next couple of days came and went without incident; everyone was occupied with their usual duties. The guys continued to help Ashley with the equipment in the barn, while Amanda worked on her project for Mr. Lawrence before starting to prepare the Monday night dinner for the crew: baked chicken with rice and vegetables. However, as she was cooking the meal, her mind drifted into another daydream involving Hank and herself.

Amanda sighed at the fantasized recollection of sitting on the counter while Hank moved in towards her. She envisioned his lips as rough, but the perceived kiss was passionate and erotic. She imagined the heat radiating from his bare chest; his hands roaming over her torso, and it heightened her arousal. She yearned for the sensation of his straining erection pressing against her, covered by layers of material. Amanda was getting warm again, and needed to release the tension pent-up inside of her again; she had to seek relief.

She looked outside the window to make sure everyone was still busy. When the coast was clear, she snuck upstairs to the bathroom, stripped naked, and stepped into the shower. The water cascaded over her flesh, and was refreshing to the touch; however, there was only one true way she could cool down. She rubbed her hands over her body; imagining they were Hank's. Amanda envisioned the careful and loving touch of the journeyman as they moved along her neck, across her shoulders, and further southward. She cupped her breasts and lightly tweaked her nipples; trying to capture the perceived sensation of Hank's mouth and tongue stimulating them to erectness.

Amanda's hands continued lower; her fingertips caressing her stomach before jumping to her legs. She trailed them along the sensitive insides of her thighs; inching closer to the region that needed to be touched the most. She was attempting to prolong the experience, but knew relief had to come soon. Amanda couldn't accept her denial for much longer. She traced her fingers along her damp folds and shivered in delight. Amanda knew it couldn't match what Hank's touch might feel like, but it was the best she could muster at the moment.

Her fingers located the swollen nub, and it cried for attention. Amanda began to massage the arousal point, and a soft moan escaped from her lips. She wished for Hank to touch her the way she needed to be touched, right at that moment. Amanda continued to pleasure herself, not wanting the sensation to end. However, she tumbled out of her dream when there was a knock on the bathroom door.

"Amanda, are you in there?" a voice asked. "Are you alright?"

The voice was one she recognized instantly, and worried if she had been overheard. Amanda grabbed a towel and wrapped it around herself before opening the door. Standing before her in the doorway, holding a half-consumed bottle of water in his hand, was Hank showing a look of concern.

"Hi Hank," Amanda said, feigning her innocence. "What seems to be the problem?"

Hank reported, "I came in to grab a bottle of water from the fridge, and saw the pot on the stove was boiling over."

"Oh shit," she exclaimed, "I forgot all about the rice I had on for dinner! The stove is ruined, isn't it?"

"I was able to catch it before it got too bad," he said. "Once I set it on another burner, I had to go looking for you. I know you're not the type who'd leave something unattended intentionally."

"No," she said. "I thought I had time to grab a quick shower before the rice was done. It was a mistake on my part."

Hank looked at Amanda and noticed her skin was flushed. He couldn't help but smirk. Amanda looked down at her feet, embarrassed.

"It looks like someone has been fantasizing about their mysterious crush," he teased.

Amanda blushed. "I'm sorry," she said, "but I can't help it. I'm warm for his form. He's got a body that just doesn't quit, and I can't help but be aroused at the mere thought of him."

Hank sniffed the air, and remarked, "I thought I detected the slight aroma of steam and sex. He must really get your engine revving."

"More than you ever could know," Amanda confessed. "If he was here right now, I would have no qualms about dropping this towel and showing him what he could have if he wanted it."

Hank chuckled. "Now Amanda, are you sure you should be talking like that around me? What would your beau say? By the way, you never told us what this guy's name was."

Amanda gulped hard. Hank was putting her on the spot, and it was making her uncomfortable. She was unsure about confessing her feelings towards him. If she did, then it could open a huge can of worms. However, if she didn't within the next few days, she could lose him forever.

"You're right," Amanda said. "I haven't revealed who he is. However, I'm unsure if he feels the same way about me as I do about him. I'd love so much to tell him, but I'm worried about any possible repercussions it might cause."

Hank placed a reassuring hand on Amanda's shoulder, and it sent a warm sensation through her body. "I can't speak for him," he said, "but if he truly does care about you, he would be supportive in your plight. I know you and Ashley talk, so she probably knows; she's pretty good at keeping things quiet. I promise I won't bother her or you about it, I respect your privacy. It's Kevin and Cecil I'm worried about. If they were to find out, they'd blab it to anyone at the bar. I couldn't trust a secret to those two if my life depended on it."

"That's why I have to be careful with what I say or do around them," Amanda said. "I don't want the whole town to know about him and I; at least, not yet."

"That's understandable," he said. "I'm sure all will be unveiled in due time, but I know the two of you are still in your infancy. There's no telling who or what might come along, and try to break up what you're trying to build."

"I must admit," she said, "it's a concern I have. With my leaving to head back to Toronto on Sunday, I'm worried some harlot might come along and steal him away from me."

Hank replied, "I'm sure he won't let that happen."

Amanda looked into Hank's eyes. "Are you sure about that?" she asked. "Long-distance relationships can be a challenge, and given his looks, I'm sure every woman within 200 miles of here will do their best sales pitch in a bid to convince him to 'go local' after I've gone."

The journeyman sighed. "Is there anything I could say to assure you he will stay committed to you, and only you?" he asked.

Amanda thought for a moment before replying, "I know you mean well, but right now the only thing that would soothe my soul is if he were here to join me in the shower for a serious make-out session."

Hank laughed. "If I knew who he was," he said, "I'd see if I could twist his arm for you. However, I should head back to the barn before Kevin and Cecil start getting any crazy ideas."

Amanda nodded. "I understand," she said. "Thanks again for taking the rice off for me."

"It's my pleasure," he said. "I'd hate for the house to go up in flames. I'll leave you to return to your 'business.'"

Hank gave Amanda a wink, and began to make his way back downstairs.

"Hey Hank," she called out to him; interrupting his progress. He turned to face her near the top of the stairs. Amanda closed her eyes, and took a deep breath. "I know this is unprofessional of me," she said, "but if he were standing here in front of me, this is what is awaiting him."

Amanda opened her towel and flashed her naked body at Hank. The vision flustered him to the point where he almost fell down the stairs, but was able to catch himself when he stumbled on the first step. Amanda giggled at the sight of Hank being affected by her playfulness, and with a wink, returned to the bathroom where she rinsed herself off, got dressed, and returned to the kitchen to finish preparing the night's meal.

~ * * * ~

By the time everyone came to the dining room for dinner, Amanda was able to salvage what was left of the rice. The side dish would have been a catastrophe had Hank not made the save earlier, and prevented the kitchen from billowing smoke. It would have caused the others to go on a frantic search for her, and might have led to a more intense line of questioning when they learned she was in the shower. It was embarrassing enough as it was when Hank caught her in mid-masturbation; however, Amanda didn't mind. If anything, she would've loved if he joined her in the bathroom to 'finish the job', but she knew better to have kept him from his duties in the barn. Plus, it would also have meant she would have to confess to Hank that he is the one who's been getting her all hot and bothered.

"Another amazing meal, as always," Cecil complimented.

"Thanks," Amanda replied. "It almost didn't happen. I was in the shower and forgot about the rice. Fortunately, Hank caught it in time before dinner was completely ruined."

Kevin noted, "It's still a commendable job, regardless."

Ashley turned to the heir and whispered, "Were you doing up there what I think you were?"

"Only to me," Amanda whispered back. "But, Hank did interrupt my train of thought when he checked on me. Unfortunately, he didn't join in for obvious reasons."

"Duly noted," Ashley said. "It must be hard to carry on like this under a veil of secrecy."

"Hank knows that you know," Amanda reported, "and he won't press you on revealing the mystery man's identity; he respects our secrecy. It's the other two we're all concerned about."

Ashley nodded. "With just cause," she said. "I hate to find out how they'll react when they do find out."

Kevin interrupted the women's gossiping. "Say, Amanda," he asked, "will you go out with your date from last night again?"

"We haven't made any official plans, but I suppose I could give him a call and ask him if he's free tonight."

Hank replied, "It couldn't hurt. I'm sure whatever you two 'crazy kids' decide upon, you'll both have fun."

Amanda smirked at Hank. She wanted to admit to him that the man she had been going on about was the man sitting across from her at the table; however, she thought better of it and simply stated, "I'm hoping so."

Cecil asked, "Have you heard back from him about Friday night yet?"

"Not yet," Amanda replied. "I meant to call him when I was at Linda's, but we got into talking about him and I plum forgot about it. I'll ask when I call him after dinner."

"Great," Cecil said, "I'd like to meet this guy."

"Me, too," Kevin added.

"I think we'd all like to meet him," Ashley commented.

"You will, in due time," Amanda assured. "It's just that he's a rather shy guy, and he might find meeting a crowd of people to be intimidating."

Ashley replied, "That's understandable. While I'm sure Hank and I can be mature about it, I'm not too sure about Mutt and Jeff over there."

Kevin accused, "That term is derogatory to all mixed breeds."

Cecil added, "And, no one is more mixed up than the two of us."

"You're not helping our case, Cecil."

"Oh, and you are?"

Hank attempted to restore calm. "Guys, guys," he pleaded. "I'm sure Amanda will introduce us to him when they're both ready to do so."

Amanda said, "Thank you, Hank. Rest assured you all will meet him when the time's right. Who knows? You might all be pleasantly surprised."

A sly grin emerged from Ashley's face, and whispered, "I think they all will be."

CHAPTER THIRTEEN

Amanda decided to pay another visit to the upstairs study, but not
to spy on Hank again. Instead, she was perusing the room's
bookshelves; looking for something that appealed to her literary
tastes. Most of the books in Gerald's collection consisted of
historical fiction; however, she was able to find a few holdovers of
Evelyn's amongst the stacks. Either Gerald didn't know they were
there, or he kept them as reminders of his departed wife.
Regardless, Amanda was in need of some evening entertainment,
and she couldn't keep fantasizing about Hank. So, as a change of
pace, she thought some reading would whittle the time away. She
decided on a romance novel her aunt used to own, and sat down in
the same chair she pleasured herself in mere days before. Amanda
was a few pages into her book when she heard a knock on the open
door. She looked up from the page, and saw the man within her
dreams leaning against the doorframe.

Amanda smiled at the visitor. "Well hello, Hank," she said. "To
what do I owe the pleasure of this visit?"

"Good evening, Amanda," he replied. "I was wondering if you
would like to take in a movie tonight."

"Does Melville even *have* a movie theatre?" she asked.

"It does," he explained, "but it's not a very big one; it only has one
screen. The building it's in used to be a paint store years ago;
however, it does the trick for our small community."

"Are the others coming along?" Amanda quizzed.

"No," Hank said, "it's just you and me."

Amanda feigned a surprised look. "Oh ho," she said, "so it's your turn to ask me out tonight, huh?"

"I just wanted to return the favour from our coffee outing last night," he said.

The heir doubted her employee. "Uh huh," she said. "Are you sure it's not just an excuse to try and lure the identity of the man I'm smitten with?"

"Would you turn me down if I said it was?" he asked.

"Hank," Amanda said, "did you forget about my little flash this afternoon? If I was willing to expose myself to you, what makes you think I would turn down your movie date request?"

A sly grin emerged on Hank's face. "I thought you might have heard back from your mystery man," he joked, "and decided to run off with him instead."

Amanda rolled her eyes and sighed. "I don't know who is worse with their inquisition," she said, "you, or Kevin and Cecil. Speaking of which, I thought you said you weren't going to press me about him."

Hank apologized, "You're right, I'm sorry. I promised not to harass you about it, and I'm reneging on my end of the bargain."

"It's alright," Amanda said. "You're eager to know, but don't worry. I'll tell everyone in due time."

"How 'due' are we talking about here?" he asked.

Amanda thought for a moment. "Well," she said, "if you guys haven't figured it out before Friday night, I'll reveal him then; he'll be joining us for our soiree to honour Uncle Gerald."

"So," Hank said, "you're planning on throwing him to the wolves, huh? You do realize you will be subjecting him to the ridicule of our group, right?"

"It is a risk, I do admit," said the heir. "However, I'm entrusting everyone will be on their best behaviour."

Hank chuckled. "Well, if worse comes to worse," he said, "Ashley will talk some sense into us."

Amanda nodded. "That is definitely true," she said.

"We'll worry about that then," Hank said. "Getting back to my original question, are you still interested in the movie tonight?"

Amanda mulled over the offer, and gave her answer. "Aside from reading," she said, "I had no other plans for tonight. Alright, let me grab my purse and we'll go."

Hank smiled. "Excellent," he said, "and I promise not to try anything funny with the popcorn bucket."

A smirk formed on Amanda's face. She commented, "You do realize I am still your employer, right? I don't think it would be proper to trick me into giving you a hand job."

The journeyman laughed. "I know it's wrong to resort to such trickery, but you can't blame a guy for trying."

The heir rolled her eyes. "Hank, I'd expect that type of joke from the others," she said. "I thought you were better behaved than them. However, while some women might jump at the opportunity to get you off, I'm going to decline. Besides, considering this is a small town, I'd rather not have word get around that I'm a slut."

"That's understandable," he argued. "Although, you could claim that living in Toronto has corrupted you."

"Do you think the people around here would buy that?" Amanda asked.

"That's hard to say," Hank mused. "However, just to be on the safe side, I suggest we keep any 'naughty flirting' to ourselves."

Amanda agreed. "While it has been miniscule," she said, "it's probably for the best. We both have reputations to uphold."

Hoping to make the early showing, Amanda retrieved her purse from her room, and the two friends were off to the show.

~ * * * ~

Amanda and Hank made their way down the aisle; checking to see if there were a couple of available seats in the cinema. After some discussion, the couple found a pair of empty chairs in the back third of the theatre. Amanda and Hank manoeuvred their way down the row and plopped down in the seats. They surveyed the rows around them, and when they thought the coast was clear, leaned into each other for a quick kiss. Amanda remarked how the screening room reminded her of a 1980's style cinema chain where they possessed multi-screen facilities, but each individual screening room was no bigger than a large closet. The conversation shifted to how much movie theatres had changed in the years since. Gone were the days of a small, slightly-sloped screening room. Today's theatres offered such frills as stadium seating, and in the rare instance, licensed facilities; where one could sample an alcoholic beverage in a lounge situated in the theatre lobby.

116

Amanda and Hank began to chat about the difference in liquor laws between various jurisdictions within Canada and the United States. The couple agreed there needed to be tougher controls, but despite them, if young people were going to drink, they would find a way to circumvent whatever laws were on the books. They noted the youth of today were attracted to the notion of binge drinking, an act where one would consume as much alcohol as possible within a short period of time, but were dismayed over the fact such actions would do incomprehensible damage to one's mind and body. Amanda sighed, and wished more people would be able to be cognizant of their actions.

Hank asked, "Have you ever had an instance where you've pushed your limits, and ended up regretting it later?"

"Only when it came to drinking in university," Amanda confessed. "I think anyone who parties while in school is bound to overindulge once in a while."

"Were you a party girl while going to school in Saskatoon?" he probed.

"I tried my best to stick to my studies," she replied, "but that's not to say I didn't show up as a date to a couple of frat parties."

"I bet you got hit on a lot at them," Hank said.

"Not really," Amanda said. "I was rather plain while I studied."

"Well," he said, "I'm glad to see you've come a bit out of your shell since then."

Amanda blushed. "Thank you," she said. "What about you; have you done anything you've regretted?

"You know," Hank replied, "in all of my travels, I didn't do anything that I was sorry for later."

"I don't believe that," Amanda said. "There must have been something you wish you did differently, or missed an opportunity you kicked yourself about afterwards."

Hank delved deep into his memory banks, and tried to recall an instance where he made a mistake he ended up paying for. Little did Amanda know there was, but Hank had repressed it for years. It was something he kept within him for years, and didn't want it to be revealed. It was part of the reason why he was hesitant to allow women to get too close to him. However, he felt comfortable around Amanda.

Hank thought, "Amanda is a good friend and trusted confidant. If it wasn't so wrong, I'd pursue things further. Maybe if I came clean about the financial backer for the farm, she'd see me as an equal instead of an employee. The thing is if I want her to take me at face value, she ought to know all of my strengths and weaknesses. Should I open myself up to her, and unveil the pain I've held inside all this time?"

He took a deep breath and was about to state his confession; however, they were interrupted by an unwelcome visitor.

"Well, well, well," a female voice crowed. "What do we have here?"

Amanda knew the voice, and it was one she had dreaded on hearing. "Why did she have to show up now," she thought, "why here, of all places?" She turned her attention to a few seats to her left, and standing before her, with a smug look on her face, was Rebecca Brimley.

She addressed her cousin with frigidness in her voice. "Hello, Rebecca," she replied. "What brings you out from your gopher hole?"

"Well, I was going to take in the movie when I saw you and one of my father's workers sitting over here, and I just had to come by and say 'hello'."

Hank explained, "Amanda and I are attending the screening as a couple of friends and colleagues."

"And, you expect me to believe that?" Rebecca doubted. "With all due respect, Hank, you are the hottest guy in all of Saskatchewan. You could have your pick of any woman in the province, and you decide to hang out with *her*?!? Quite frankly, you could do much better."

Amanda was ready to leap out of her seat, and get in Rebecca's face; however, Hank hand a firm grip on her arm. "Is there any particular reason you've decided to cause this scene now?" Amanda spat.

Rebecca tut-tutted her cousin. "If you're trying to win me over," she said, "you're failing."

"That goes both ways," the heir retorted.

"Anyway," Rebecca continued, "I just wanted to inform you I've been speaking with my lawyer regarding Dad's Will. You should be hearing from him in a couple of days."

"Your case doesn't have a leg to stand on," Amanda said. "Mr. Mitchell said the document was airtight."

"My lawyer and I see it differently," Rebecca pronounced with confidence. "Daddy's farm will be back in the possession of its rightful owner."

Hank glared at Amanda's cousin. "That will be up to the courts to decide," he said.

"We shall see," Rebecca clucked. "Have fun on your 'date' tonight, you two, and on your group outing Friday night."

Amanda's jaw dropped. "How did you know about Friday night?" she asked.

"Amanda," Rebecca said, "you're not in the big city right now; this is Melville. If someone is going to make plans, eventually, word is going to get out."

Rebecca gave the couple a wave, and with a cackling laugh, made her way to her seat. Hank turned to Amanda and saw the angered look on her face. "Well, that was a complete mood-killer," he quipped.

"That woman makes me so mad," the heir fumed. "I could chew metal and spit nails."

Hank gave Amanda a comforting pat on her hand. The gesture calmed the heir. "You do realize you're going to have to call Leonard, and let him know what just happened," he said.

"I have all intentions to," Amanda said, "but we shouldn't let that self-absorbed bitch ruin our evening. Let's try to enjoy the movie together. We should also warn the others of Rebecca's threat. If she's true to her word, our night to honour Gerald will be ruined."

"We don't know if she will, or not," Hank said. "For all we know, it might be an idle threat to keep us on our toes."

120

"I hope you're right," she said, "but considering the way Rebecca's mind works, I'm worried."

The couple did their best to be entertained, but the whole time Amanda looked at the back of Rebecca's seat; daggers in her eyes. She knew Rebecca would reveal herself sooner or later, but she had chosen to do so at an inopportune time. Amanda wanted to make her pay, but little did she know Rebecca Brimley would not be finished yet.

CHAPTER FOURTEEN

After the movie, Hank and Amanda decided to stop into the Timmy's to grab a coffee. He had an ulterior motive: attempting to simmer Amanda down, who was still fuming from Rebecca's grandstanding at the theatre.

Amanda complained, "I should have known Rebecca would crawl back out from whatever rock she was under, and try to stir up shit. Why did she do it now all of a sudden?"

Hank mused, "She probably got wind of you heading back to Toronto on Sunday, and wanted to file her claim just before you left. That way, you would've flown back, and not known about it until it was too late."

"If that's the case," the heir fumed, "it shows what type of low-life she is. She doesn't care about the farm. She doesn't care about the good people who have worked for my uncle. All she gives a shit about is the money she could sell it for. Fuck, for all I know, she'll probably unload it to some potash mining company, or maybe the developers for some oil pipeline who'll destroy everything Uncle Gerald and you guys have worked so hard on."

Hank took a sip from his coffee. "Amanda," he said, "it's a concern for all of us; regardless of who owns the property. If Rebecca got her hands on it, it would just expedite the process. What you need to do is call Leonard, let him know of Rebecca's song-and-dance tonight, so he can contact Mr. Mitchell. If need be, we'll rally our troops, and see if we can earn enough support for Gerald's side."

Amanda played with her coffee cup and sighed. It was supposed to be a perfect night out for Hank and her, but it was ruined because of her egocentric cousin. Amanda didn't want to wake up from the dream she had been experiencing the past few days interacting with him. First, the coffee date the previous week, followed by Hank checking up on her in the bathroom when she almost ruined dinner, and then his invite to the movies tonight. Amanda believed he was all the man she could ever ask for, and she couldn't fathom what her life would be like when she stepped on the plane in Regina in a few days, and return to her advertising executive job in Toronto. How could she; all she would be thinking about is the journeyman she had been fantasizing about. It was a notion that saddened Amanda; she would be waking up from her dream world soon, but she didn't want it to end.

She said, "I'm afraid she might cause more trouble after I've left on Sunday."

"We're all aware of the type of person Rebecca is," Hank said. "Gerald hinted at it after every time Rebecca visited him. But, we all knew he wouldn't give in to her. Leonard's doing his best to uphold Gerald's belief; however, everyone at the farm and I will stand by you and Leonard throughout all of this."

"I appreciate that, Hank," Amanda said, "but I'm afraid she won't stop at just the farm. Rebecca has a vindictive streak, and she's had it in for me every since I was given the farm instead of her. The thing that worries me the most is what she might do to screw me over, and if she plans on doing what I think she will…"

Hank took Amanda's hand into his. "Amanda," he said, "I assure you, as much as she might try to drive a wedge between you and everyone in town, there is no chance in Hell we would let her do that. You mean too much to the staff. I know it sounds crazy for me to say this, because we met a few days ago, but there is only one woman who ought to be the rightful owner of your uncle's farm, and it's not Rebecca Brimley."

Amanda smiled. "I'm glad you feel that way," she said. "I just hope the courts share the same sentiment when the trial is heard."

Hank looked into Amanda's eyes and saw the light shine within them. He was captivated by her beauty, but had to restrain his emotions. "I can't say I know what the judge will say when he announces his decision, " he said, "but if Leonard, Linda, the rest of the staff, and I had our way, we wouldn't rule against you. We are all committed to you as our friend and supervisor. While we know a few days from now you'll be on a flight heading back to Toronto, I want you to know that a little part of all of us will be stowed away in your carry-on bag."

"Thanks for the support," she said. "It means the world to me. I wish I could stay longer, but Mr. Lawrence is insistent I return to work on Monday. It sucks that I have to, though. You all have been great to me. It makes it hard to leave."

The couple finished up their coffee, and headed back to the farm. With a storm brewing in the form of Rebecca, they felt the others should be prepared for what was about to head their way.

~ * * * ~

Ashley came out of the guest house to find Amanda and Hank pulling into the driveway. She had a look of concern on her face when she saw Amanda slam her car door. She asked, "Amanda, what's wrong?"

Hank stated, "We have a situation, Rebecca's back. Rally the guys and tell them to meet us in the dining room."

Ashley nodded at her co-worker, and rushed into the guest house to gather up Kevin and Cecil. The five converged in the dining room a short time later where Amanda and Hank would report the news.

Hank began his speech. "The reason why we've called you here is because we ran into Rebecca tonight, and she's starting to stir up shit," he said. "She informed Amanda her lawyer will be notifying her in the next few days. We suspect Rebecca is going to bring Gerald's Will before the courts in a bid to wrest the farm away from Amanda and into her possession."

"She can't do that, can she?" Kevin asked. "Gerald's Will was pretty airtight."

"We all know it was," Amanda stated, "but Rebecca is claiming Uncle Gerald was not of the right mind when he composed the Will; hence, why she's dragging it into legal proceedings."

Cecil inquired, "Is there any chance her bid will be successful?"

"We doubt it," Amanda answered, "but, if her intentions are the same as they have been, and the courts rule in Rebecca's favour, she plans on selling the farm, and you all will be out of a job."

Hank added, "That's why we wanted to give all of you the head's up. We suspect this is going to turn into a character assassination of both Gerald and Amanda. Should it come to that, we need each and every one of you to testify to their good name. We can't have Rebecca tarnish the reputations of the two people we've grown to know, love, and respect."

"You know you have my support," Ashley replied.

"I'm in, as well," Kevin added.

Cecil concurred. "Me too," he said. "This place is our home, and we have become a family together. I'll be damned if Rebecca tries to break us up."

Amanda answered, "Thanks, everyone. That means a lot to me."

Cecil had a confused look on his face. He asked, "The one thing I don't get is how Rebecca ended up running into the two of you?"

Hank explained, "Amanda and I decided to go to take in a movie tonight, and Rebecca noticed us in the theatre. So, she came up to us, and started her shit."

Kevin interrupted, "Wait a minute, you two went to the movies tonight and didn't invite us? I thought you liked having us around."

Amanda defended, "We do, but Hank and I wanted to do something alone together."

"But, what about this mystery man you've been going on about the past couple of days?" Kevin continued. "Does he know you're cheating on him by going out with Hank?"

Amanda and Hank looked at each other; then, looked at Ashley. The female farmhand nodded at them both; telling them it was time to come clean.

"I have to confess something," Amanda said. "When I went out on my coffee date the other night I wasn't out with a mystery man. I was out with Hank."

Cecil attempted to wrap his head around what was being said. "Hold on, hold on," he interrupted. "You were out with Hank, and you *weren't* cheating on the mysterious stranger?"

Ashley encouraged her co-worker to put the pieces together. "Come on, Cecil," she mocked. "You're almost there."

Kevin clued in. "You mean, Amanda and Hank are an item?" he asked.

Amanda looked at Ashley again, and again, Ashley gave her a non-verbal vote of confidence. The heir turned to Hank, and made her confession. "I know this is wrong for me to say this," she said, "but I've been harbouring an interest in you for a few days now."

Cecil asked Ashley, "And, you *knew* about this?"

"Damn, you two are thicker than molasses," Ashley scolded. "I know you guys don't see it, but you have to be blind not to notice what a hot-looking guy Hank is. Women around town have been clamouring to be with him ever since he started working here. Shit, if we didn't work together, I'd have thrown my hat into the ring."

Hank was dumbfounded by the bold admissions by the women in the room. "So, let me get this straight," he asked, "both Amanda and Ashley had been looking at me as something more than a colleague?"

"Hank, sweetie," Ashley explained. "You get a lot of women around here hot and bothered. But, unlike them, I respect the kinship you and I share. I don't want to jeopardize that for a possible romantic relationship between you and me."

Unsure of what to say about her blunt admission, Hank could only stammer out, "Thank you, Ashley. I respect your honesty." He then turned to his supervisor. "And what about you, Amanda?" he asked. "Are you like all of these other women Ashley is talking about, or do you respect me like she does?"

Amanda gulped hard. She was being put on the spot with the revelation. However, knowing she had dug herself into a hole already, the heir attempted to climb her way back out of it. "I didn't want to say this in front of everyone," she said, "but Rebecca is subconsciously forcing my hand into it." Amanda took Hank's hand into hers, and she looked deep into his blue eyes. "I'm trying to be considerate of the whole employer-employee relationship, but the minute I first saw you, I was caught by how gorgeous you were. However, unlike these 'other women' who Ashley says fawn over you, I wanted to be sensible about things. I wanted to get to know you better, I will admit to that, but I did it without any intentions for anything sexual."

Ashley mumbled, "Bullshit."

Amanda glared at her female employee, and then continued her speech. "I wouldn't blame you if you wanted to file a sexual harassment lawsuit against me, I would deserve it with my admission. But, I want you to know that I enjoy your company, Hank Acker, and I wish we could continue to get to know another, and see what happens from there."

Hank was at a loss for words. He didn't know what the bigger shock was: the fact everyone in town saw him as eye candy, or the admission by his employer that she would like to enter into a relationship with him. Hank had some stirrings within him ever since his first coffee date with Amanda, but had kept himself in check, concerned she might fire him if he told her how he felt. Now, Amanda had come clean about her feelings towards him. Should he confess his feelings, as well?

Amanda looked at the journeyman with hope in her eyes, but was concerned over his hesitation. Did she just open her heart, only to find the feelings weren't mutual? She was taking a huge gamble in saying what she said, not just to Hank, but in front of the others. Amanda was setting herself up for a huge fall, and she worried about how rough the landing was going to be.

Hank looked at Amanda, caressed her cheek, took her hand into his, and lightly kissed the back of it. "Amanda," he said, "I didn't know how to say this, but the feelings you share for me, I have towards you, too. I think back to our first time in Timmy's together, and I remember how beautiful you looked that night under the light of the moon. I knew that night, you were someone I could enjoy spending time with."

Amanda's jaw dropped. "You do?" she asked.

The journeyman nodded. "Like you," he continued, "I was hesitant about admitting this because I knew I worked for you, and I didn't want to find myself out of a job. I didn't want to turn my back on the farm because I respect my co-workers and Gerald's legacy too much. That's why I didn't say anything. However, knowing what I do now, I would like to pursue such a relationship with you, Amanda Bellamy; that is, if you want to."

Amanda's face lit up with the brightest smile. "Of course, I want to," she said.

The heir and journeyman fell into a warm embrace, and gave each other a sweet kiss. Kevin and Cecil made gagging sounds to mock the new couple. Ashley shot them a stern look, and attempted to restore order. "As much of a happy moment this," she said, "we can't lose sight of the fact that Rebecca is coming after us, and she might say or do something that will break our little group apart. If she finds a weakness in any of us, she'll try to exploit it to her

The Prairie Fire Within

advantage. We all need to be a united front when battling her; regardless if she tarnishes Uncle Gerald's character, tries to break Hank and Amanda up, or attempts to drive a wedge between any of us. We cannot let Rebecca win; we've worked too hard to get where we are today to have her tear us apart."

Kevin commented, "Rest assured, Ashley, in the good name of Gerald Brimley, we will not let everyone down."

The other employees agreed with Kevin's sentiment. Amanda was relieved to hear she had everyone's support, but she was still worried about Rebecca's next move. Did Rebecca harbour ill-will towards her own father because he had shunned her recommendations to sell the farm and retire in his final years? Would she be malicious in her attempt to discredit Gerald just to get what she wanted? Amanda wasn't sure what was about to transpire, but she knew Rebecca would not rest until she got what she believed was rightfully hers. It wasn't a matter of how Rebecca would do it; she tipped her hand at the movie theatre. It was a matter of when she'd execute her plan.

130

CHAPTER FIFTEEN

Amanda awoke on Tuesday morning after a restless night's sleep. She spent the night tossing and turning in her bed; worrying about when Rebecca would put her plan into action. Amanda wished Hank had spent the night in the same bed with her; not for any sexual activity, but to hold her as she slept. Having him by her side would have soothed her soul. It was a surprise he didn't suggest it, since everyone else on the farm knew about their newfound relationship after the meeting the previous night. But, it would have been for the best in the event Rebecca and her lawyer showed up to serve the subpoena. It would have added more fuel to the smouldering hatred between Rebecca and the others.

After a quick shower, Amanda got dressed and headed down to the dining room where the others were getting ready to sit down to breakfast. When she arrived, everyone greeted her with a smile. Hank had made a coffee run to Timmy's, so they were enjoying their 'morning Joe' with the steaming bowls of oatmeal Ashley had prepared.

Hank handed Amanda her beverage, and gave her a kiss. "Good morning, Amanda," he said.

"Good morning, dear," the heir replied, "and thank you."

Kevin and Cecil returned to their jovial gagging motions at the behaviour of the newly-announced lovebirds, but a stern look from Ashley forced them to stop again.

"I see the boys are mocking our relationship," Amanda observed. "They didn't give you a hard time about it last night, did they?"

Hank replied, "Just the usual crap a pair of jealous, younger brothers would do."

"We're not jealous," Cecil defended. "We're happy for the both of you."

Kevin added, "We'd just prefer not to have to endure your public displays of affection while we're trying to eat."

"I'm sure you two boys would be singing a different tune if it was one of you with a beautiful woman instead of me," Hank said.

Ashley came in from the kitchen and commented, "Kevin or Cecil with a beautiful woman? She'd have to be blind for that to happen."

Cecil accused, "Really, Ashley? Was that even called for?"

"Oh, come on," Ashley said. "You know I'm just busting your chops like a sister would. I'm sure you'll both find someone special someday."

"I hope it will be soon," Kevin said, "because I'm getting tired of having to wake up in the morning to Cecil's bodily noises."

"I'm doing the best that I can, Kevin," Cecil replied. "But, those antacid tablets can only do so much on one's digestive system."

"Then lay off the late-night snacks," Kevin retorted. "I swear, if I have to hear another popcorn fart from you, it'll be the death of me."

Hank turned to Amanda and smirked. "You got to love family breakfast conversations," he replied.

Amanda asked, "Can we please talk about something else before I lose my appetite? Are you all going to continue working in the barn today?"

Cecil replied, "Actually, the guys and I were going to break out the irrigation tractor and water the fields. We haven't gotten much rain the past few days, and we want to make sure the seeds we planted germinate."

Ashley asked, "We should be due for some showers soon, shouldn't we? The system that threatened us a couple of days ago might've been the start of a few days of rain."

Kevin corrected, "Yes, but it held off so we could finish the planting."

Hank posed, "Do you think you can check the latest weather report, Amanda?"

Amanda got up from the table to fetch her laptop. "I'm on it," she said. A few keystrokes later, and they had their answer. "Clouds are rolling in," Amanda announced. "But, a minimal chance of rain is forecast; only a 30% chance of precipitation."

Kevin noted, "Well then, we better fill up the tanks, and get out there after breakfast. Those seeds will blow away in the wind unless they take root."

Cecil bemused, "I don't know what's worse: not getting enough rain, or getting too much."

Amanda asked, "But, those freakish thunderstorms don't usually pop up until later in the summer, don't they?"

Hank explained, "Normally, they don't. But, we've been getting warmer weather earlier in recent years. Thunderstorms can pop up at any time from Victoria Day until almost Thanksgiving, and out here, when they do, they're vicious ones."

Ashley chimed in, "I remember the last one we had last year; it was a real gasser. Cecil and I were in the barn while Gerald and Hank were out in the fields. There was so much rain it felt like a monsoon had blown in. They had to floor it in their combine and get back to the barn to take cover. By the time all was said and done, there had to have been a couple of inches of rain on the ground. The fields were flooded, and we were afraid the whole crop would be ruined. But, we were still able to salvage a reasonable yield; it wasn't much, but we got by."

"Hopefully," Cecil stated, "it won't be as bad this year, and we'll be able to bounce back. We think you can be our good luck charm."

Amanda laughed. "I don't know about that," she said, "but I'm sure Uncle Gerald is smiling down on all of us, and wants us to do the best we can to make this a productive season."

Hank smiled, "I know he's already helped turn my year around."

Kevin bemoaned, "Okay, I'm getting sick again. Get a room, you two."

Cecil cautioned, "Don't give them any ideas. Remember, Hank sleeps a couple of doors down from us."

Ashley remarked, "And, what makes you two think they'd do their business in the guest house? Amanda's room is perfectly fine for any canoodling, should they decide to take that step; which, I might add, is none of our business."

Amanda stated, "Yes, and before this goes any further, Hank and I have a request for you two."

134

"What is it?" Cecil asked.

"We ask the both of you not to make a big deal of our relationship," she said. "Around the farm is fine, but we don't want anybody coming after Hank or myself because they object to us being together. Of course, having Rebecca see us together at the movies last night might make that a moot point. She's probably got the whole town gossiping about us by now."

Kevin assured Amanda, "Don't worry; we'll keep this under our hats. Hank is seen as the most eligible bachelor in the entire Prairies, and there might be some women who would be jealous of the one who took him 'off the market'. I don't know who exactly they might be, though, since I don't see Hank much off the farm."

Cecil offered, "Maybe they all congregate around him whenever he goes to Timmy's for a morning coffee run. He'd be more of a reason to wake up in the morning than the coffee."

Hank laughed. "Unfortunately," he said, "there's only one of me. They can't have me as a double-double."

Ashley said to Amanda, "Could you imagine the idea of there being two Hanks?"

Amanda teased. "I could date one," she said, "and you could date the other. It'd be win-win for 'Uncle Gerald's girls'."

Cecil asked, "But, how would the two of you know which Hank is the one you're involved with?"

Ashley pondered the situation. She suggested, "Maybe we could tie different coloured ribbons around their..."

Hank objected, "Hey, let's not get into discussing my man region at the dinner table. There has to be some level of decorum."

Amanda continued, "How about red for my Hank, and green for Ashley's?"

Ashley laughed. "Well, they do say 'Green is the colour'," she said.

"You two are terrible," Hank complained.

"We can't help it if we have a similar taste in men," Ashley defended.

Amanda added, "You would think you would be flattered to have two women bestowing your 'virtues'."

Hank sighed. "Perhaps," he resigned, "but remember, there are two other guys here at the table who are feeling left out."

Cecil replied, "Thanks, Hank."

Ashley countered, "Yes, but Kevin and Cecil aren't as easy on the eyes as you are; no offense, guys."

Kevin rolled his eyes. "We'll try not to be offended," he said, "but, it won't be easy."

Amanda suggested, "Before this escalates any further, we better finish breakfast, and get these guys out watering the fields."

Cecil joked, "Oh sure, send us out into the fields while we're hurt. Maybe we can irrigate the crop with our tears?"

Ashley slapped Cecil's arm. "Oh, stop it you two," she said. "You know we still love you both."

Kevin grinned. "Those are hollow words now, Ashley," he said, "but we'll try to find it in our hearts to forgive you."

136

The guys gathered the empty dishes and brought them to the kitchen. Kevin and Cecil had disheartened looks on their faces, but couldn't hide the grins that were forming. They knew the banter was all in good fun, and there was no ill-will meant towards them. While Kevin and Cecil got to work in the kitchen, Hank and Amanda shared a moment with each other in the dining room.

"I hope they don't give you a hard time in the fields," she worried.

"They won't," Hank said. "After we retired to the guest house last night, they congratulated me on our new relationship. They said, 'Out of all the women in town I could have chosen, they were glad I picked you.'"

"That's reassuring," Amanda replied. "I'm sure they have seen the stream of women who have beaten a path to the guest house in a bid to make you fall for them."

"There have been some interesting ones who came by in the past," he admitted, "but none of them could really 'get' me. They always had unscrupulous intentions, but I saw through them all. I came to the realization the only person who I would want to spend time with is a woman who likes me for me; not for what I could give them."

"You can't blame them for wanting to try," she said. "You are easy on their eyes. They are attracted to the complete package: your eyes, your smile, your body, and your, um…"

Hank was confused. "My… what?" he asked.

Amanda blushed. "I can't believe I'm saying this," she said, "but, your endowment."

Hank looked at Amanda with his eyebrow quirked. "My *endowment*," he asked again. "You like my 'endowment'?"

Amanda smiled and waved her hand in front of her. "Yes," she repeated, "your endowment. I've seen the type of 'package' you possess, and if women knew about it, I can't blame them for wanting to know you in that sense."

Hank released Amanda from his grasp. He had a dejected look on his face. "I see," he said. "I should get out to the fields. Kevin and Cecil are waiting for me."

Amanda asked, "What's wrong? Is everything alright?"

Hank replied, "I have to get to work." He walked over to the door with conviction; a fragment of his heart broke away with each step. He paused for a moment, and turned to Amanda. "You know," he said, "I thought you were a special woman; different from all of the women who have come through my life. But now, after what you just said, it makes me wonder if you're like all of the others."

Amanda was dumbfounded. "What are you talking about?" she asked. "How am I 'like all of the others'?"

"Good day, Miss Bellamy," Hank stated, as he slammed the door behind him.

Amanda stood in the dining room in shock. She didn't know how to react to Hank's outburst. "What did he mean I'm 'like all the others'?" she wondered. All she had were questions, but soon they were replaced with grief. Amanda feared the worst; the man of her dreams may have started to walk out of her life.

CHAPTER SIXTEEN

The rest of the day Amanda was in a funk. Her heart was in disarray over the events of that morning. She attempted to comprehend the end results. "Hank and I were starting a wonderful relationship together," she thought, "but now, he's backing away. What did I say or do which made Hank change his attitude towards me?" Amanda replayed the tape over and over in her mind, but she couldn't pinpoint the exact moment. The emotional pain was preventing her from doing so. The only thing she did know was whatever happened, it was her fault, and she wished she could do something to correct it.

She wanted to talk to Hank about it, but he was out in the fields with the other guys. When Hank left, he gave the impression he wanted nothing to do with her; citing she had become 'like all the other women' in town. Amanda kept asking herself, "How could it be possible to have changed in a second? How could he go from liking me one moment to hating me the next?" Amanda needed to talk to someone, but with the boys out watering the crops, there was only one other person on the property she could turn to. She wiped away the tears, and made her way to the barn.

When she entered, she found Ashley tightening a bolt on the processor. She didn't notice the broken hearted redhead approach in near-tears.

Amanda's voice was unsteady; the pain and confusion evident. "Ashley," she asked, "do you have a minute?"

Ashley looked up to find a dishevelled woman. "Amanda," she responded, "what's wrong?"

"I… I don't know," a sobbing Amanda responded, "but I think I might have lost Hank."

Ashley set down her tools and rushed to Amanda's aid. "Oh my God," she asked, "what happened?"

Amanda recounted the events of the morning to the best of her recollection. Ashley listened with an attentive ear; comforting her friend when she was on the verge of breaking down.

"The thing is," Amanda stated, "I don't even know what it was that changed his mind. How could someone tell you they want to be with you one moment, and then not wanting anything to do with you the next?"

Ashley nodded. "I think I know," she said.

"What is it?" Amanda asked. "Tell me what it was I said or did, so I can beg Hank for forgiveness."

"I'm sorry, sweetie," Ashley replied. "Hank swore me to secrecy."

"Please, Ashley," the heir pleaded. "I have to know what I did wrong."

Ashley patted Amanda's hand. "The only thing I can tell you is there is more to Hank Acker than you know," she said. "It's something he only allows certain people he trusts to know."

Amanda was confused. "What do you mean 'allows certain people he trusts'?" she asked. "I thought I was someone he trusted."

"I guess he hadn't felt comfortable enough to share it with you yet," Ashley stated. "He was building that trust with you, but when you said what you did, he believed he couldn't trust you. It's the same reason he doesn't trust the majority of women in town; they know of his secret, you don't. The only advice I can give is you have to do your best to win him over as a friend. If you're able to do that; then, *maybe* he will share it with you. But, until that time, he will be distant."

Amanda was becoming desperate for answers. "Ashley," she cried, "I beg of you, isn't there something you could say to him to make him see I didn't mean what he thought I said?"

The farmhand sighed. "I'll see what I can do," Ashley said, "but, I can't promise anything. It's something Hank will have to do on his own volition. However, if you want to help your case, I suggest you don't press the issue. It will drive him further away, and whatever chance you might have to win him back will be lost forever. I know it won't be easy, and it will be painful. But, you have to trust me on this."

Amanda fought through her sobs, and agreed to do what Ashley suggested. If it meant the possibility of getting Hank back in her life, she had to follow her instructions. However, there was a small flicker of the pilot light deep in her soul. Amanda did not want it to be extinguished. She needed Hank, and if it meant rebuilding everything she had torn down by her actions or words to get him back, she would do it. He meant that much to her. The only problem was the unknown factor: did she still mean anything to him?

~ * * * ~

That night's dinner was an uneventful meal. The women were concerned Kevin or Cecil might say something at the table which would've made an already volatile situation worse. Much to their relief, they remained quiet. They wondered if Hank told them what had happened while they were watering the crops, but the men were noticeably silent. It was a painful experience for Amanda to go through. She wanted to apologize to him for something when she wasn't even sure what she did wrong. However, for the good of her slim chances, she kept quiet about it. Once the meal was done, and the dishes were put away, a sorrowful Amanda headed to her room. Sensing she wanted some alone time to let her emotions out, the others retired to the guest house for the evening.

Hank returned to his room after his shower to find Ashley standing in the doorway. She had a disapproving look on her face, and was demanding answers.

"I hope you're proud of yourself, Hank," she stated.

"I have no idea what you're talking about," the journeyman replied.

"You know damn well what I'm referring to," she accused. "You owned the heart of a wonderful, sweet woman, and you broke it in two because of your pride."

"She broke mine with what she said, Ashley," he countered. "I thought she wasn't like all of the other women around town. I thought she liked me for who I am; not for what I could provide."

"She doesn't even know about that," Ashley said. "You never told her about it. Now, she's up in her room crying her eyes out because of something she unknowingly said that pissed you off."

"She said she liked me for my 'endowment'," Hank announced. "How am I supposed to react to that?"

142

Ashley laughed. "You realize that means more than one thing, right?" she said.

Hank chuffed. "What else could she have meant?" he said.

Ashley grabbed Hank's towel, yanked it away from his torso, and pointed at his genitals. "She was talking about your cock, Hank," she proclaimed. "She liked your big dick."

The journeyman blinked. "How did she know about that?" he asked.

"Hank, sweetie," Ashley explained. "You're a smart guy, but there are times when you've got to be the dumbest fuck out there. Come with me." Ashley took Hank's hand and led him to his bedroom window. "You see that window over there?"

"Yeah," Hank snorted, "it's the window to Gerald's study. What about it?"

"Have you ever thought about the possibility of someone looking out of that window and seeing something more than they bargained for?" she said.

Hank started to realize what Ashley meant. "Wait a minute," he asked. "You mean to tell me Amanda was spying on me through that window?"

"She only did it once that I know of," Ashley stated. "She was reading or working up there, and saw you come out of the shower."

The journeyman replied, "So, what you're saying is, she peeped into my room, saw me drying off, and caught a glimpse of 'Little Hank'?"

Ashley scoffed. "Trust me, honey," she said, "it's not little. You're packing some serious meat there."

Hank was confused. "But, who told her about that vantage point?" he asked.

A smile formed on Ashley's face. "Who do you think," she answered.

Hank blinked. "You did?!?" he exclaimed. "Why would you do that?"

"You may think of me as a sister," Ashley explained, "but, I'm still a woman. I like Amanda; she's a good woman. If I could help her spend a lonely night on the Prairies looking at some of the 'fine scenery', it's all for the better."

The notion began to sink in for the journeyman; his pride and ego left the woman he loved shattered. Hank sat his naked self on the edge of his bed, and buried his head in his hands. "Oh my God," he bemoaned, "what have I done? I've broken Amanda's heart because of a misunderstanding. Does she know the reason why I reacted the way I did?"

"I alluded to it," Ashley said, "but I didn't tell her. I know you prefer to keep this between yourself and the people you trust."

"Thank you, Ashley," he said.

"However," she continued, "I do think you should tell her. It's the only way the two of you could smooth things over."

Hank doubted the advice. "Do you think she'll understand my plight?" he asked.

Ashley sighed. "I don't know, sweetie," she said, "but, I want you to remember one thing: Amanda is leaving for Toronto in a few days. If you have any shot of smoothing things over with her, you need to sit down with her one-on-one, and tell her everything. I know it won't be easy because she's still broken up over what happened, but if you're going to win her back, you *must* patch things up with her before she leaves."

Hank nodded. "I'll try to talk to her before we head out tomorrow night," he said. "I'm hoping we can sort everything out so we can all enjoy the night together. I'd hate for this misunderstanding to spoil Gerald's night."

Ashley smiled at the naked man before her. "You know, Hank," she said, "somehow, I have a feeling Gerald will be guiding you two back together tomorrow night."

CHAPTER SEVENTEEN

Amanda awoke the next morning; her pillow damp from the tears she had shed the night before. She hoped there was something she could do or say to win Hank back. However, she worried if she might have been too late. She hadn't seen Hank since the night before, and for all she knew, he went out to the bar after dinner. Amanda feared another woman might have entered the picture, and was able to sweet talk her way into his heart. "No," she told herself, "Hank wouldn't do that. He said all of the women around here were alike; only after him for one thing, just like he thinks I am now."

Amanda needed to compose herself before she headed down to breakfast. If she looked dishevelled, it would incur a barrage of questioning from Kevin and Cecil. She wasn't ready to hear from them. This was something she and Hank needed to talk about one-on-one, but would the journeyman be willing to accept the olive branch Amanda wanted to extend?

After cleaning up her face and getting dressed, Amanda made her way to the dining room. All of her staff, save for Hank, sat at the table awaiting her presence; they all had concerned looks on their faces. They knew she had a rough night, and they worried she wouldn't be the same woman they had met a week and a half before. Amanda took her seat, and she had a solemn look on her face. Her heart was still in pieces from the day before. She took a deep breath, and looked up from her spot. It was then she recognized the plate before her was stacked with heart-shaped Saskatoon berry pancakes.

"Good morning, sweetie," Ashley said. "We had a feeling you had a rough night, so we whipped up a special breakfast for you."

Kevin handed Amanda her coffee: a large double-double from Timmy's. He said, "I would have gotten you an extra-large, but I didn't think you would have been able to drink it all."

Amanda was still feeling depressed. "Thank you, everyone," she said. "But, I'm not sure I'm worthy of such preferential treatment."

"That's nonsense," Cecil said. "We think you're more than worthy. You're as much a part of our family as Gerald was, and we wanted to show you how much you mean to us."

"You didn't have to go through all this trouble," Amanda said.

"Technically, we didn't," Cecil continued. "However, since none of us want to feel Hank's wrath, we all pitched in."

Amanda was surprised. "Hank put you up to this?" she asked.

Hank emerged from the kitchen with a bottle of pure maple syrup. He was wearing a chef's hat and a frilled apron with 'Kiss the Cook' printed on the front. He said, "I was wondering when the guest of honour was going to show up. I was afraid I had laboured over a hot griddle for nothing."

Amanda was still attempting to process the information she had heard. "Hold on a second," she said. "Hank cooked breakfast this morning?"

"I sure did," the journeyman confirmed. "I remembered how you said you loved Saskatoon berry pancakes from when we had them last week, so I whipped up a special batch for you. I was able to find a couple of heart-shaped cookie-cutters in one of the drawers, and I used them as the moulds for the pancakes."

"That was very thoughtful of you, Hank," she replied, "but I thought you said to me yesterday..."

"Actually," Hank interrupted, "I was hoping you and I could talk about that after breakfast, alone."

Amanda nodded, understanding it was a private matter between the two of them. However, it didn't seem like it was private if Hank had dragged the others into the fray. Amanda cracked a small smile; knowing this was the opportunity she wished for since the incident a mere 24 hours earlier. Yet, she was hesitant; Hank had turned on her in the blink of an eye the day before. She worried she might say or do something to have him push her away again. Regardless, she had to wonder why he had changed his tune.

Around the breakfast table, everyone discussed their plans for their outing later that night. Ashley cautioned Kevin and Cecil not to go overboard on their drinking. They assured her they would limit their alcohol intake, but she remained skeptical. Amanda noticed Hank was looking over at her; she hoped breakfast would be over soon, so they could discuss matters in private. She didn't know he was debating about whether he should tell her his secret. Ashley thought he should, but it was a matter of his comfort and trust levels.

"Would she be able to forgive me for pushing her away?" Hank thought. It was an internal conflict which weighed on his heart. He had to explain himself, but Hank worried Amanda wouldn't understand his plight.

Everyone devoured their pancakes in earnest, but Amanda was hesitant. The heir saw that Hank and Ashley were concerned over her lack of an appetite.

Ashley asked, "Are you alright, honey? You've hardly touched your food."

"I'm fine," Amanda said. "It's just, Hank went through a lot of trouble to make these for me, and I don't want to destroy his handiwork."

"He'll be disappointed if you don't eat at least one," Ashley explained. "You know he did it because he cares about you."

"It didn't seem like he did yesterday," Amanda whispered. "He just turned on me; all because I said something that set him off."

Ashley patted Amanda's hand. "I talked to him about it last night," she said, "and I suggested he try to make amends as soon as possible."

Amanda's face showed both shock and embarrassment. "You told him about my attraction to his," she stammered, "you know?"

Ashley nodded and pleaded with Amanda to eat her breakfast. Not wanting to make things worse than they already were, Amanda dug in. They turned out to be the best pancakes she had ever tasted. The Saskatoon berries exploded in her mouth every time she bit into one. It brought back the memories of her youth, and she came to the realization: with the farm in her possession, she could come back 'home' any time she wanted. "Rebecca, be damned," Amanda thought. "I'm going to fight for everything I've earned; whether it is the farm or Hank." Amanda looked up at the journeyman, who had been observing her from across the table. She flashed a smile after downing another bite. "My compliments to the chef," she said.

The rest of the meal went smoothly. Once it was over, Ashley got Kevin and Cecil to gather up the dishes and the three of them went to work while the moment Hank and Amanda dreaded had arrived. It was time for the two to iron out their differences.

"I wish there was a way we could discuss this without the others overhearing us," Amanda said.

"There is," he said. "Come with me."

Hank took Amanda's hand and led her out to the porch. They didn't notice Ashley looking out the window, watching the couple walk out the front door, and a smirk forming across her face. They didn't know Ashley had an inkling there would be some 'making up' taking place, but didn't say a thing for fear the boys might cause trouble.

~ * * * ~

Hank sat down on the porch swing, and patted the area beside him. Amanda was hesitant to join him, unsure about how things were going to develop.

"Join me, Amanda," he begged, "please?"

The heir reluctantly took her seat, but attempted to keep a bit of distance between her and the journeyman, for fear he would turn on her again.

"I figured this would be easier for us to be alone instead of having prying ears eavesdropping on us," he said.

"I think Ashley would be able to keep Kevin and Cecil in line," Amanda stated, "but this is probably best for our own peace of mind."

"Yes," he said, "I wanted to talk to you about
my behaviour yesterday."

"I was wondering what the hell was going on?" she replied.
"Ashley told me I had said something out of line, but she didn't
elaborate on what it was. Regardless of that, I want
to apologize for what I said."

"I should be the one apologizing to you." Hank said. "When you
said you liked my 'endowment', I thought you were alluding to
something else."

Amanda was confused. She didn't know what Hank meant at first.
She was giving him a compliment about what he possessed
between his legs; a natural-born gift in its own right. However, she
wondered what else it could have meant. It did not dawn on her
until Hank nudged her in the right direction.

"The only other thing I can think of is..." Amanda's voice trailed
off.

A wry grin emerged upon Hank's face. "Let's just say my trousers
aren't the only thing that's big and loaded," he said.

Amanda clued in. "Hold on," she said. "You mean to tell me that
you're rich?"

Hank looked down at his boots and nodded. "Yes, Amanda," he
confessed. "I was the winner of a huge lottery jackpot about four
years ago."

Amanda blinked. "But, if that's the case," she asked, "why are you
working here instead of living off of your winnings?"

Hank took a deep breath. "I've always been raised as someone
who should work for a living," he explained. "I didn't want
to stop doing that after I claimed my cheque. Unfortunately, when
word got out about my windfall, everyone started coming out of

the woodwork. Co-workers started begging me for money. Everywhere I turned, people wanted a slice of the pie. Don't get me wrong, I helped out my family, and a small group of charities; I like giving back, but it was becoming too much. So, I packed up a few of my belongings, and started touring around the Prairies."

"So," Amanda asked, "wherever you tried to settle down, your secret would get out. People would start hounding you, and you would shuffle off to somewhere else?"

"That's right," Hank confirmed. "It wasn't until I got to Melville where I truly felt I could keep a low profile. When I was comfortable enough, I told your uncle and the others about my secret. However, as you know by now, Kevin and Cecil were never ones to keep their mouths shut. Word started to spread around town, and the next thing I knew, every gold-digging woman in this part of Saskatchewan came a-calling. To them, I was a piece of arm candy that could double as their sugar daddy."

"But, when that happened," Amanda asked, "why didn't you pull up stakes again, and move somewhere else? It must have been tempting for you to fall into the same pattern as before."

Hank took Amanda's hand in his and lightly passed his thumb over the back of it; giving it a subtle massage. He sighed, as he continued his confession.

"I thought about it," he said, "but I had developed a close bond with Gerald and the others. We all saw he needed all the help he could to keep this farm afloat. It was Ashley who convinced me to stick around. I never had much of a family after I left home. When Gerald accepted me with open arms, I finally felt I had been accepted as part of one."

"That's why all of you consider me like a sister," she said. "Uncle Gerald thought of me like one of his own children, and you all saw him as a father."

"Exactly," Hank said. "However, since his Staff was more of an adopted family, we're akin to your stepbrothers and stepsister."

Amanda laughed. "That's a relief," she said, "because I'm not sure I'm comfortable with the whole incest notion. But, what about this secret backer you said you would help line up to give us a loan?"

Hank sighed. "Amanda," he said, "I'm the backer. And, the money I gave isn't a loan."

The heir was shocked. The man she had developed feelings towards – but feared she had lost – wasn't just willing to save their relationship, but the farm, as well. The revelation of his secret capital enabled Hank to hold a stake in the farm with his generous donation. Because of this, any weird feelings the two originally had regarding an employer-employee relationship were eliminated. Hank would be considered an equal to Amanda. It was a notion that relieved the heir. He could be entrusted to run the operations of the farm after Gerald's niece returned to Toronto. However, there was part of Hank that wished Amanda wasn't leaving in a few days time. Little did he know that deep down, she wished the same.

CHAPTER EIGHTEEN

Over the next couple of days, there was a developing romance between the newly-formed partners after their reconciliation. Hank and Amanda would exchange loving glances at the dining room table, and while Kevin and Cecil were reluctant to, they learned to accept it. The heir explained to them that the journeyman was the man who helped save the farm from financial instability in the short-term. It would still be a few weeks until they would hear back from the Ministry of Agriculture about their claim for assistance, but for the time being, Hank was willing to float them the necessary funds to keep the operations running.

While Hank and Amanda enjoyed each other's company, there was the looming factoid of the heir's sojourn back east. Awaiting Amanda's return was the resumption of her life as an advertising executive. She didn't want to leave the farm, knowing Rebecca was destined to strike at any moment. Although, she had faith in Leonard and the members of her new family to fight for the cause, there would be a void left behind, and it could only be filled by Hank. Amanda would have loved to bring her new love to Toronto with her; however, she needed him here to make sure things continued to run smoothly. Hank was not only a prime investor, but also an operations manager alongside Ashley. His absence would leave Ashley in charge of not only handling the day-to-day management, but having to control both Kevin and Cecil upon her own, and that was a task unto itself.

Amanda's upcoming departure was not lost upon Hank either. The woman he loved would be leaving his life in a few days, and it would leave an empty space in his heart. Like Amanda, he had no experience in a long-distance relationship; yet, he was willing to do his part in attempting to make it work. However, he worried about being forgotten once Amanda returned to her normal routine.

He had to do something to make sure she would stay as loyal to him as he vowed to be to her. He remembered the misunderstanding from earlier in the week, and after some soul searching, he decided to put his risky plan into place.

After that day's lunch, he made sure Ashley, Kevin, and Cecil were busy doing the dishes. He requested Amanda to join him outside. Once she arrived on the porch, he took her hand in his, placed his finger against his lips as a symbol for the two of them to be quiet, and he led her towards the barn. The couple climbed up a ladder to the barn's hay loft. The first thing Amanda noticed was a blanket laid amongst the mounds of straw. Hank invited Amanda to take a seat upon the blanket, and she carefully sat down.

"I hope you don't have any allergies," he said.

"None of the sort," Amanda replied. "I don't think I would've spent my summers as a child here if I did. Why did you bring me up here?"

Hank took Amanda's hand in his, and looked into her eyes. "I know you'll be leaving in a few days to return to Toronto," he said, "and I'm concerned you will get too busy with work that you'll forget about all of us here in Melville."

"I will admit it is a concern of mine, too," she said. "But, I have no intentions of leaving all of my life behind again. In the time I've been back here, I've been able to be reconnected with my roots, and have met some wonderful people in the process. They took me in, and made me remember that no matter where I am, I will always have a family here; including a wonderful man I met and fell in love with."

"You mean I have some competition for your heart?" Hank joked.

Amanda smacked her lover's arm. "I'm talking about you, silly," she replied. "There is no other man I want to be with."

"I feel the same way about you," he admitted. "I didn't think I would ever find a woman who would love me for me. Now that I have, I don't ever want to lose her."

Amanda caressed the journeyman's cheek. "You're not going to lose me, Hank," she said. "The physical distance apart will be hard, but I will come back to visit the first chance I get. After all, this is my farm, and I have to make sure things are running smoothly."

"It's not just your farm, Amanda," Hank corrected. "It's our farm: yours, mine, Ashley's, Kevin's, and Cecil's. Yes, your name is on the title, but we all work together to make sure this family business is a productive and profitable one. That being said, I want to make sure the rightful owner doesn't forget what she's leaving behind."

"And how do you propose to do that?" she asked.

Amanda looked up at Hank and saw his blue eyes twinkling in the sunlight. He interlocked his fingers with hers, and slowly guided her hand to his mouth, and kissed the back of it. Hank brushed the hair out of Amanda's eyes so he could see the shimmering emerald pools before him. She shied away from his touch at first, but he cradled her face in the palms of his hands; turning it towards him. Hank brushed his thumb across her lips, and she fought the urge to take it into her mouth.

Amanda was yearning for his kiss; she wanted to feel his lips pressed against hers. He would not disappoint as he moved in and granted her wish. She tasted the remnants of the mid-day meal upon his lips. Not only was there sweetness to the kiss, but warmth, as well. Amanda parted her lips; inviting his tongue to enter. Hank leaned in, and snaked it across her teeth; commencing a tango with hers. She welcomed the attention, but believed he would pull away if things were to become too heated.

Hank undid the ponytail Amanda had her hair in, and let her auburn locks falls down to her shoulders. He ran his fingers through it; enjoying the feel of the strands in his hands. The sensation of Hank's hands massaging her scalp was relaxing and stimulating to her. Amanda never had her scalp tended to in such a manner before, but it was a feeling she enjoyed. She wondered why she had gone without such a relief all of her life.

"That feels nice," Amanda said.

"There's a lot more where that came from," Hank replied.

"Then please," she insisted, "don't stop."

Hank moved behind Amanda and began to rub her shoulders. "You have quite a bit of tension pent up within you," he said.

"The stress of the past couple of weeks has played havoc on my psyche," Amanda admitted. "Is there any way you could alleviate it?"

"I'll try my best to," the journeyman said.

Hank worked his magic, kneading the flesh through the fabric of her shirt to the best of his ability, but it didn't appear he was having much success. Picking up on the cue, Amanda turned her head, kissed his lips again, and began to unbutton her shirt. Her heart pounded in a frantic rhythm; she couldn't believe she was removing clothing for Hank so soon after their tiff. "I hope this isn't another one of my daydreams," Amanda thought. "I don't think I could take it."

Once the buttons were undone, Amanda removed her shirt; exposing a teal-coloured bra. She tossed her shirt to the side and brushed her hair aside to allow Hank to have better access to her shoulders and back. He placed his hands on her flesh, and let his fingers do the work; rubbing and kneading the muscles in a bid to relieve the pent-up stress within them. She sighed with contentment as she felt the tension melt away.

However, not to pass up the opportunity, Hank lowered his head and kissed the back and sides of Amanda's neck. The feeling sent electricity along her spine. A soft moan escaped from Amanda's lips, as she tilted her head; allowing Hank better access for his ministrations. She was surprised when he took things further by nibbling upon her earlobe. "Maybe Hank is trying to get me in the mood?" Amanda said to herself. "No, it can't be; he's going to leave me hanging after getting me all worked up. I'm sure that's what's going to happen."

When Hank finished the massage, Amanda turned around to face him. Her chest was heaving; her breath possessed a slight raggedness because of his attention. He cradled her face again, and kissed her full upon the lips, but this time, there was a hint of smouldering passion within it. The feel of his lips upon hers sent a jolt of electricity through her body, and she welcomed it.
She wanted to return the favour for making her feel this way, and she knew how to do it. Amanda began to unbutton Hank's shirt at a meticulous pace; taking in his musky scent as she went along. She pushed the shirt off his shoulders and down his arms. Amanda ran her hands along his muscular torso; feeling every inch of his chest and taking all of him in. Amanda didn't want to believe this was actually happening, but in the event it wasn't a dream, she wanted to give him the same pleasure he gave her.

She lowered her head and kissed his chest; then manoeuvred her way behind him. Amanda straddled the area of the blanket behind Hank and began to massage his shoulders. She noticed he was feeling as tense as she was.

"It looks like I'm not the only one who is feeling stressed out," she said.

"To say I have had a lot on my mind the past few days would be an understatement," he admitted.

A sly grin emerged upon Amanda's face. "Well," she said, "I'm going to have to fix that, aren't I?"

The heir continued to knead and manipulate the flesh. She was more impressed with how well-developed his shoulder and back muscles were. Remembering how wonderful the feel of his lips felt on her neck, Amanda leaned in and began to kiss the side of his. Hank didn't react at first, but she was able to make him moan his approval when she began to nibble his earlobe.

"Do unto others as they would do unto you," she said.

"It is the fair thing to do," he agreed.

Amanda's sly grin turned into a devilish one. She said, "Then, I hope you think what I'm about to do is 'fair'."

She moved her hands around Hank; giving him a hug, while she trailed kisses down his spine. Amanda then slid them southward, and began to unbutton the fly of his jeans. Hank inhaled deeply when she slid his zipper down, and slid her hand inside. She noticed he was already becoming aroused, and began to massage him through the fabric of his boxers. Another moan escaped from Hank's lips. He wanted her to set him free, but she was enjoying her fun. Amanda remembered back to her daydream of Hank teasing her in the kitchen. Now, it was time to turn the fantasy into a reality.

Amanda slipped her hand underneath the waistband of Hank's underwear, and she heard him exhale. It was her first opportunity to touch the massiveness firsthand since she observed it through his bedroom window. Amanda trailed her finger along the shaft; feeling its length, and cooing as she tracked every inch it possessed. Hank begged her to set him free, and with a twinkle in her eye, she obliged; moving the denim and polyester down from his hips with some assistance. Hank's arousal sprang from its hiding place and Amanda was able to get her first 'up close and personal' look at it.

She trailed her fingers up and down its full length. "Six, seven, eight," Amanda counted in her head. "My God, he is so huge!" Hank shivered at Amanda's touch, but warmed to it. She wrapped her hand around its base and began to stroke it. It was a slow pace, but Hank enjoyed the massage. He swallowed hard as she continued to run her clenched hand up and down his hard shaft. Amanda's ministrations unleashed the beast within him, as he forced her hand away from his arousal. Hank turned and pounced upon his partner; forcing her back onto the blanket.

He began to kiss Amanda with a feverish passion and hunger. If she wanted him that bad, she was going to get all of him, and then some. Hank unfastened the belt looped around Amanda's waist, and began to undo the fly to her jeans. However, instead of teasing her like she did to him, Hank slid his hands underneath the waist, and pulled them off along with her panties. He retrieved the lingerie from the discarded pants and inhaled the traces of her sweet scent. The aroma turned him into an animal, as he spread Amanda's legs apart, and began to kiss his way up the insides of her thighs.

A moan escaped from Amanda's lips as she felt Hank's lips and tongue on her sensitive flesh. She whispered for him to keep going, but Amanda worried Hank might not grant her wish. His breath was warm on her skin as it inched closer to the region that was begging for his touch. He stopped for a moment and inhaled deeply; taking in her scent. Hank was at the doorstep, and Amanda was inviting him in.

Hank offered a light lick at first; sampling Amanda's sweetness. The feel of his tongue against her sent another bolt of electricity through her body. He licked her once again, and she moaned her approval. Hank was toying with Amanda; he was pushing her buttons, and he was going to enjoy tempting and teasing her. He shifted his head and gave her exposed nub a soft kiss. The feel of his lips on it made Amanda buck in a reflex reaction. An even louder moan emanated from her; she knew she had to have him inside her, but Hank wasn't going to grant her that reward right away.

He continued to run his tongue up and down her quivering folds; teasing her nub with his mouth on occasion. Then, Hank took things to the next level; he slipped a finger inside of her. Amanda gasped at the feel of something foreign penetrating her arousal, but it was not the appendage she hoped for. However, she believed this was a prelude for the sweet reward that was still awaiting her. Hank slid his digit in and out of Amanda; her sweet juices coating his finger. His tongue focused on her nub; it swept, tickled, and flattened against the sensitive area. The combined sensation made Amanda squirm and rock her hips; inviting more attention from her lover.

"More," she begged, "I want more."

Hank granted her wish by slipping a second finger inside of her. Amanda winced at the feel of being stretched, but she was appreciative of it. She knew she had to be in order to accommodate what was still awaiting her; what she wanted ever since she laid eyes on it. The question was would Hank be willing to grant her desires after everything they had been through during the previous four days? He had shied away from her before. Amanda wanted him to carry through this time around. She knew he needed it as bad as she did. She knew it would be a matter of time, but she wanted that time to be now.

Amanda ran her hands through Hank's hair; forcing his head deeper into her warmth. She was urging him to make love to her with his mouth, and he lapped every ounce of her. Each lick of his tongue, every stroke of his fingers brought Amanda closer to the first wave. She bucked her body against him as he brought her higher than she had felt before. She moaned her approval at Hank's cunnilingus. Then, she felt herself tumbling over the edge.

161

She gasped, and sat silent as her orgasm shook her very being. As the sensations overtook her, she panted and pulled Hank's lips to hers for a deep, hungry, passionate kiss. Amanda tasted herself on his lips, it was sweet with a bit of a tang, but it was all for her lover. She looked into Hank's eyes and noticed they had darkened to a deeper shade of blue. He was ready, and Hank knew what he had to do next.

Hank positioned his naked body to sit on the end of the blanket, and took Amanda's hand. He guided her into his lap and steadied her as she got comfortable. His rigid arousal brushed up against hers, and brought an erotic sensation to them both. Amanda took hold of Hank's shaft and carefully guided its tip towards the part in her folds. There was a slight discomfort at first when the swelled head penetrated the walls, but the two lovers grew accustomed to each other's dimensions. Soon, they would become one, and Amanda's dreams would come true once and for all.

Amanda sat on Hank's arousal; allowing it to fill her inside. It had been years since she had been with a man like this. She was excited and scared at the same time, and it was conveyed in her eyes when she looked at Hank as he entered her. Hank caressed her cheek, and assured her he would be gentle with her. Hearing his words calmed her down to the point where both of them felt safe and ready to take the next step.

"Are you ready?" Hank asked.

"In my mind," Amanda confessed, "I've been ready for days. Are you?"

"Considering I'm buried inside of you," Hank replied, "I'd say I am."

Amanda giggled as Hank winked at her. She began to rise up and down in Hank's lap; allowing his arousal to enter and retreat in a slow, rhythmic motion. Another moan escaped from Amanda's lips, but one also emanated from Hank's. The two lovers rocked in

162

unison as they looked deep into each other's eyes,
then brought their lips together for an erotic kiss. Hank gripped
Amanda's back for support; roaming over her torso, but noticed
her brassiere was still clinging to her body.

"You must feel restricted with that on," he said.

"I am," she replied. "Would you be so kind to remove it for me,
please?"

Hank said nothing further as his hands located the clasp to the
garment, and began to unhook the fasteners. A few moments later
the back strap fell open and Hank's hands began to massage the
exposed flesh. He hooked his thumbs underneath the shoulder
straps and peeled the lace from Amanda's torso.
Her breasts breathed in the surrounding air, and her nipples stood
erect. A sly grin emerged on Hank's face, and Amanda nodded to
grant her lover permission to give them some proper attention.

Hank brought his right hand around to cup Amanda's left breast.
She moaned her approval to his touch; his fingers brushing against
the pert areola. He slid the nipple between his index and middle
fingers; lightly pinching it. Amanda gasped and moaned at the
rough ministration. She was enjoying the attention, and she
reciprocated by taking more of Hank into her. He moaned for his
lover as they delved deeper into their passionate escapade.

Not to be satisfied with Hank's touch, Amanda arched her back;
inviting him to sample more of her breasts. Hank took his cue, and
lowered his head. He curled his tongue around the aroused areola,
and took it into his mouth. Amanda moaned as she felt Hank
suckle upon her teat and nibbled upon it. The sensation
sent another pulse of energy through her. She brought Hank's lips
back up to hers for another deep kiss, and she dug her nails into his
back. Hank groaned at the rough foreplay, but bucked his hips
upward to match the increased rhythm Amanda was dictating.

The Prairie Fire Within

Amanda moaned for her lover, urging him to take her to the
pinnacles of ecstasy. Hank continued to stroke in unison with her.
He gathered her into his arms, and laid her back onto the blanket.
Amanda repositioned her legs, and wrapped them around his waist.
She begged him to make love to her. She didn't care about
the fact she was leaving for Toronto in two days time. For her,
there was only the here and now. Amanda did not want to be
anywhere else; she wanted to be making love to Hank, and her
wish was being granted.

Hank's body began to tense up. He sensed he was close to his
climax, but attempted to hold off. He wanted to release at the same
time Amanda did. Her body noticed he was close, and it drove her
towards her own orgasm. The two lovers' pulses raced in unison as
they brought each other towards the apex. Their
bodies shuddered together, and at that moment, there was no
misunderstanding, there was no retreat; only two people brought
together in a passionate union unlike anything either of them had
experienced before.

Hank collapsed on top of Amanda, and stayed there until he could
catch his breath. She rolled him over onto his back, and noticed his
breath was as ragged as hers. The two lovers curled up in each
other's arms, and noticed the morning sun shining through the
wooden planks that made up the barn's walls.
Their naked bodies were beaded with sweat, but at that moment,
they realized they were meant to be together. Hank had found his
mission: no matter where Amanda would be, he would be with her
in a spiritual, emotional, and physical sense. Amanda made no
complaints when he made the vow because she knew she had
found the man she wanted to spend her life with, and she would be
there with him, and for him, no matter where she was in the world.

After what seemed like an eternity, Hank suggested, "I suppose we
should return to the others."

"It's probably for the best," Amanda agreed. "They're probably
wondering what's taken us so long."

164

Hank pulled up his jeans and buttoned his shirt. "I'm thankful neither Kevin, nor Cecil came in here looking for us."

Amanda brushed a few strands of hay from her hair. "Ashley would've told them to leave us be. I hope she didn't see us escape into the barn. If she did, I'm sure she'd want to know all of the juicy details."

"Considering how she has been one of our biggest confidants, I have a feeling she knew this was where we were headed."

Amanda straightened her clothes in a bid to conceal their wrinkled look. "We should both grab a shower before we start the rest of our day," she said. "I don't want to go out to the bar tonight smelling of sex."

Hank nodded. "That's understandable," he said. "I'm sure if anyone detected my 'scent', they'd start asking questions like who was the lucky lady, was she any good, and other intimate details I don't want to divulge."

Amanda rubbed her arm, unsure about the answer to her next question. "How was I then?" she asked.

Hank smiled and gave her a soft kiss on the lips. "You were amazing," he said.

She blushed and said, "Thank you. I was nervous, since I haven't been with a guy in years."

"You were absolutely incredible," he assured. "I hope there will be more instances like this in the future."

Amanda smiled. "I hope so, too," she said.

~ * * * ~

Amanda and Hank attempted to sneak out of the barn, and head to their respective homes to freshen up for the day ahead. Hank was able to make it into the guest house without a problem, but Amanda entered her residence to find Ashley sitting on the stairs leading to the upper level. A smirk formed on her face.

"Well," Ashley said, "look what the cat dragged in. If what I presume happened, I hope you two remembered to use protection."

Amanda exhaled. "Believe me," she replied, "had I known it was going to go that route, I would've waited until after you and the guys had gone to bed."

A sly grin emerged on Ashley's face. "So," she pronounced, "the two of you ended up 'doing the deed'. You do realize I'm going to hound you for details about your encounter."

Amanda blushed, and the aroma of the encounter still lingered. She was embarrassed she had been found out, but of all the people who learned of her afternoon with Hank, she was glad it was Ashley. Amanda excused herself to head upstairs; wanting to grab a shower to freshen up. Ashley waited in Amanda's room until she was done. Amanda returned with a towel wrapped around her, and was drying her hair when the interrogation began.

"Tell me everything, and don't leave a thing out," Ashley said.

Amanda responded, "First off, let me just say, sex with Hank is more than I could ever have imagined. He was thoughtful, caring, and passionate. Hank is the type of lover a woman could only dream about."

Amanda went into detail; recounting the clarification of the two lovers' earlier misunderstanding, followed by the passion which transpired in the hay loft. Ashley felt envious and aroused by her friend's description. However, she remained reserved in Amanda's presence.

"This is going to make things interesting when we all go out tonight," Ashley said.

"I know," Amanda agreed, "which is why we have to keep things quiet when we're together at the bar. I think I can trust Hank; he doesn't seem like the type who'd have loose lips."

Ashley put her hands on her hips, as if she were insulted. "Are you suggesting I might say something if I got too tipsy?" she accused.

"No," Amanda said. "I think you can hold your liquor. I'm worried about what I might say if I have one too many. That's why I want you to try and keep an eye on me tonight."

"Shouldn't that be Hank's responsibility now?" Ashley said, with a wink.

"You'd think," Amanda replied, "but my main concern is Kevin and Cecil. Since this will be my first time out with them, they might keep buying me drinks as a friendly gesture."

Ashley nodded. "And you're afraid they will get you so wasted, you might inadvertently announce that you and Hank knocked boots in the barn," she said.

"Exactly," Amanda said. "I was afraid yesterday that I had lost him forever. Now that I have him back, I don't want to lose him again because I said something stupid."

Ashley patted Amanda on her back and assured her. "Don't worry, sweetie," she said. "I'll make sure nothing bad happens at the bar tonight. Hey, I was the one who got the two of you back together, wasn't I?"

"You did," Amanda said, "and I have to thank you for that. I'm not sure what it was you said to Hank, but it worked wonders."

"Oh," Ashley answered, "I just had to clarify some shit for him. Like most men, they can be rather clueless when it comes to certain interpretations."

Amanda laughed. "Hank might be clueless," she said, "but he sure knows how to work me over good."

The two women continued to talk about Hank, and how Amanda was perfect for him. However, they both knew they had to be on their guard tonight. Rebecca was still lurking in the shadows, and Amanda had a sinking feeling her cousin was about to strike again sometime before the day was done.

~ * * * ~

The two lovers would not cross paths again until a few hours later when everyone sat down to dinner. They exchanged glances at the table, but Kevin and Cecil appeared to be oblivious to it. Their respective showers helped shield the afterglow the couple had after getting acquainted with the barn's hay loft. Only Ashley knew of their tryst, and she made sure not to say a thing for fear of any repercussions that might befall Amanda and Hank in the aftermath.

"Have you heard from Leonard and Linda about tonight yet, Amanda," Cecil asked.

Amanda said, "I know Leonard is still coming tonight, but I'm not sure if Linda will be tagging along. You know; the whole 'finding a sitter for Nate' factor."

Kevin laughed. "Maybe they could get Ashley to watch over the little guy tonight," he said. "She deserves a break from watching over Cecil and me."

Ashley said, "And have you two run amok at the bar tonight? I don't think so. I have full intentions of keeping my eye on the both of you. Besides, I don't trust you two around Amanda tonight."

Hank raised his eyebrow at her comment in surprise. "What makes you say that," he asked.

"This is the first time Amanda will have been out with us in this setting," Ashley explained, "and I'm afraid these two yahoos are going to keep buying her shooters all night long; trying to get the poor girl drunk."

Cecil protested Ashley's claim. "Amanda hasn't had much of a chance to let her hair down since she got here," he said.

Kevin added, "Aside from a coffee date with Hank, and the movie night gone wrong, she needs a chance to unwind. We promise we won't go overboard on buying her drinks tonight."

Amanda thought, "If you only knew how much Hank turned my crank in the barn, you wouldn't think I was so wound up." She would then say aloud to Kevin, "As much as I appreciate your intent, we can't have any of us go completely overboard tonight. Don't forget, a certain relative of mine is still plotting her move, and I'm concerned she might strike tonight."

"That's a little presumptuous," Kevin said. "If Rebecca's lawyer is going to serve you, he'd do it here at the farm; not at some bar where it would cause an altercation of some sort. You've heard what they say about liquid courage."

Hank agreed. "Kevin does have a point," he said. "I wouldn't be surprised if by the time all of us went out, he'll be knocking on the front door. That is, if Rebecca is that conniving enough to pull such a stunt."

The enclave further discussed the possible scenarios when Rebecca Brimley might conduct her attack. Would her lawyer knock on the door when everyone was getting ready for their soiree? Would he serve the papers when everyone was busy tending to their daily chores? Or, would Rebecca stoop so low as to leave the nasty surprise for them when they returned from the bar. All of them plausible, but not one was definitive. They all agreed whatever Rebecca had in store it shouldn't ruin their plans for the evening. Tonight was about one man; the one who brought them all together. It was their turn to honour his memory and legacy, and they would not allow his disgruntled offspring tarnish it.

CHAPTER NINETEEN

The darkening skies overhead foretold of an impending rain shower; something the farm was in need of to help the corn crop. However, in the back of everyone's mind was a storm of a different sort, the one which was brewing in the form of Rebecca Brimley. They all suspected it would blow in soon; they didn't know when. Amanda kept a tentative ear towards the front door; hoping the impending 'knock of Doom' would not come. Rebecca had warned her earlier in the week about an upcoming visit by her lawyer. She was convinced she had documented proof Gerald was not of sound mind when he composed his Will. Should her claims be successful, the farm Amanda spent the past week on would fall into Rebecca's hands, and in all likelihood, be put up for sale to the highest bidder.

The notion brought a chill to Amanda's soul. She enjoyed spending the days on the property, getting to know the people who had worked for her uncle, including the man named Hank Acker. A smile emerged on her face at the thought of her lover. It had been a roller coaster of emotions she experienced when it came to him: the initial interest, the budding romance over coffee, the uncertainty when there was a misinterpretation of something that was said, and the culmination with the events in the barn a few hours before. Amanda wasn't going to let Rebecca take all of it away from her. She had the support of Hank and the others; they were willing to fight in the name of Gerald Brimley.

The next couple of hours passed, and no undesired visitors came to the residence. Rebecca must have decided to wait in the grass a while longer. Amanda figured her cousin would strike when they least expected it. That left few options on the table. Either

Rebecca's lawyer would leave the Summons on the door when everyone was out at the bar, or he would be brazen enough to serve the papers at the establishment. She doubted the latter would occur; however, knowing Rebecca was a vengeful person, Amanda would not put it past her. Rebecca exuded a smug confidence when she discovered Amanda and Hank were out on a movie date earlier in the week. Would she take it one further and have her lawyer serve Amanda in front of everyone in a bid for public humiliation? The heir pondered, "Rebecca wouldn't stoop so low, would she?" The thoughts played in Amanda's mind, but she knew she had to ignore them. She wasn't going to let her cousin ruin her fun tonight.

As everyone left the dinner table to get ready they all had an expression of concern on their faces. They knew Rebecca was waiting until the right moment to slither out from whatever rock she was hiding under. Amanda urged them not to fall victim to Rebecca's mind games, citing the fact Rebecca would do anything to ruin their planned evening together. They all vowed to have as much fun as possible, but what was lying in the wings played heavily on their minds. Rebecca was getting to them; she knew it, and Amanda knew Rebecca loved every moment of it.

~ * * * ~

Amanda rooted through her closet, trying to find the perfect outfit for the night's outing. She would decide upon a flirty spaghetti-strapped pink slip dress over a plain red T-shirt. She decided to wear her hair down instead of tying it back in a ponytail for a change. Amanda slipped on a pair of red pumps to complete her ensemble. She gazed at her outfit in the mirror and thought she looked good. The only thing missing was the arm candy she would be bringing with her, but he would appear in due time. Amanda grabbed her purse and waited out on the porch for the others to show up.

Fifteen minutes later, the first member of the guest house arrived. Amanda was confused at the individual's appearance. She worried it might have been Rebecca's lawyer, but they would have been more formally attired. Instead, a woman approached. She sported brown hair, which hung just beneath her shoulders. Her outfit consisted of a stylish shoulder-sleeved teal dress with a hem slightly above her knee and matching heels. The woman wore a light layer of makeup, which accentuated her cheekbones. Amanda looked at her funny; trying to determine who she was. She didn't recognize the woman's identity until she spoke.

"Sakes alive, Amanda," she said. "You look like you're dressed to break some hearts tonight."

Amanda blinked in astonishment when it became clear who the person addressing her was. "Ashley," she asked, "is that you?"

Ashley nodded in acknowledgement.

"Holy shit, girl," Amanda added. "You look amazing."

Ashley smiled. "Thanks," she said. "I decided to spruce myself up tonight for the occasion."

"Have the guys ever seen you like this before?" Amanda inquired.

"Not really," Ashley said. "Usually when I hit the bar with them, I'm in a tasteful shirt and jeans. But, I figured since I'm going out with a party girl from the big city, I needed to step up my attire for the night."

"The boys are going to be tongue-tied when they see you all dressed up," Amanda commented.

Ashley laughed. "Honey," she said, "they'll be speechless when they see both of us. Not so much Hank, since he's seen you in considerably less than that."

It was Amanda's turn to laugh. "Who knows," she said. "Maybe if he plays his cards right, he'll get an encore in my room tonight."

Kevin was the next to appear. He wore a stylish gray shirt and khaki pants. He saw the women on the porch and approached them.

"Good evening, Amanda," he said.

"Good evening, Kevin," the heir complimented. "You look nice tonight."

"Thanks," Kevin replied. "Who's your friend?"

Ashley whispered to Amanda, "He doesn't know it's me? I could have some fun with this."

Amanda whispered back, "I'll play along, but whatever you do, go easy on him." She turned her attention to Kevin and said, "This is my friend, Courtney. We attended the University of Saskatchewan together."

Kevin shook Ashley's hand. "It's a pleasure to meet you, Courtney," he said. "Did you have the same major as Amanda did?"

"No," Ashley said. "Amanda was studying for her Bachelors of Commerce in Marketing while I was going for my M.B.A. But, we were in a couple of first year classes together."

"You have your Masters?" Kevin asked.

"Not quite yet," Ashley said. "I still have a couple more classes to complete before I get my degree."

"They say those last couple of courses are the toughest," he commented.

"That's what I'm worried about," Ashley said, "but I'm sure if I put my nose to the grindstone, I'll be wearing my cap and gown in due time."

Cecil exited the guest house and made his way to the others. He was decked in a green dress shirt and black pants.

"My God, Cecil," Amanda said. "I hardly recognized you without a ball cap on."

"Thank you, Amanda," he said. "I wanted to look my best for our outing tonight; even though it's just to the local bar."

"You look wonderful," she complimented.

Cecil recognized his co-worker was flirting with the woman with them. "I see Kevin's trying to get his game on early," he remarked.

Kevin stammered. "I am not," he said. "I was just talking to Amanda's friend."

Ashley extended her hand to Cecil. "Hi," she said. "I'm Courtney."

Cecil shook her hand and introduced himself. "I'm Cecil," he said. "Are you one of Amanda's friends from Toronto?"

"No," Ashley explained. "We went to school together up in Saskatoon. When she got back to Saskatchewan earlier this week, she called me up and asked if she and I could meet up. What she didn't tell me was she was working with two attractive guys."

Amanda giggled. She said, "If you think these guys are hot, wait until you see *my* date for tonight. He'll be in your dreams in an instant."

"I can hardly wait to meet this guy you've been going on about," Ashley replied. "The way you describe him makes him sound like an Adonis."

Amanda smiled. "Don't worry," she said. "You will."

The last member of the group emerged from the guest house, and Amanda's face immediately lit up. Hank was adorned with a light blue denim shirt and dark dress jeans. A pair of brown leather cowboy boots enveloped his feet. The handsome man smiled when he saw Amanda beaming at him. He walked up the porch steps, and took Amanda into his arms. They shared a soft kiss while the others turned away embarrassed.

"It took you long enough to get here," Cecil said.

"I'm sorry," Hank apologized, "but I wanted to make sure I looked good for my special lady."

"I swear," Kevin said, "this guy was in his closet for so long, you'd think he was trying on everything he owned."

The journeyman chuckled. "I couldn't decide to go with the white cowboy hat or without," he said.

"You look very handsome tonight, honey," Amanda said.

"Thanks, sweetie," he said. "You're looking pretty hot tonight yourself."

176

Amanda blushed. "Thanks," she said.

Ashley looked Hank up and down; taking him all in. "Damn girl," she said. "You weren't kidding when you said he was a looker. You lucked out big time."

Hank turned to Ashley and smiled. Unlike Kevin and Cecil, he recognized who she was. Ashley winked at him to let him know they were messing with the other guys.

Amanda introduced the two co-workers "Hank," she said, "this is my friend from university, Courtney. Courtney, this is *my* Hank."

Hank extended his hand to Ashley. "It's a pleasure to make your acquaintance, Courtney," he said.

"The pleasure is all mine," Ashley replied. "Let me say on first appearance you two make a wonderful couple, and I'm glad you both found each other."

"Thank you," Hank said.

"Shall we make our way to the bar then," Cecil asked.

The five made their way to the vehicles and prepared for the night ahead. Amanda and Hank rode in one car, while the others rode in Kevin's. Amanda laughed when she saw Kevin and Cecil argue over who would open the door for Ashley.

"It's so funny to see the guys behave like this," she commented. "They have no idea 'Courtney' is Ashley."

"I can't say I blame them," Hank said. "They usually see her with her hair tied back and in overalls. Tonight, Ashley looks like a beautiful woman."

"You really think she's beautiful?" she asked.

"From an objective standpoint, yes," he said. "However, she can't hold a candle to the vision of beauty sitting beside me."

Amanda slapped Hank's arm. "Now you're just sucking up," she accused.

The journeyman chuckled. "After what we've been through the past couple of days," he said, "I need to suck up all that I can."

Amanda winked at her man. "I think you made your penance this morning in the barn," she commented.

Hank chuckled. "Darn," he said, "and here I was hoping to sin again with you later."

A mischievous grin emerged on Amanda's face as the two cars pulled out of the driveway. Little did everyone realize when they left, there would be a nasty surprise awaiting them when they returned.

CHAPTER TWENTY

The two cars carrying the motley crew from the Brimley farm pulled into the parking lot of the local watering hole in Melville. It was a small establishment, but when Amanda and her staff walked in, everyone turned their heads to notice. Most of the patrons were tastefully dressed, but none of them were to the nines like the five were.

Cecil said to the others, "I think we might be a tad overdressed."

"Nonsense," Ashley said. "They haven't seen an attractive group of people grace this place before."

Hank whispered to Amanda, "They have, but not with us looking the way we do tonight."

The five found a couple of tables together, and took their seats. They left a couple of chairs open in case both Leonard and Linda were able to attend the night's festivities. A waitress came by and took everyone's order for the first round of drinks. The girls ordered a couple of mixed drinks for themselves. Kevin and Cecil both ordered a Pilsner, while Hank opted for a special concoction some people on the Prairies enjoyed, 'Beer and Clam.'

Amanda gagged at Hank's order. "You drink that stuff?" she asked.

"Once in a blue moon, I do," he replied. "I'm more of a straight beer guy."

"I should hope so," Amanda stated." A good pint is one thing, but mixing it with Clamato juice is repulsive."

"It is an acquired taste," Cecil said. "Do they serve the combination down east?"

"Thankfully, no," Amanda explained. "The only time you see Clamato blended with alcohol is in a Caesar. Then again, what doesn't go well with vodka?"

"I know what really goes well with vodka," Ashley said, "*more* vodka."

Everyone laughed at Ashley's comment. Kevin and Cecil whispered to each other, debating about what type of person 'Courtney' might be when she was drunk. Would she be sociable, or a wild party girl who might end up in either of their beds? They had no inkling she was the same woman who normally kept them in line every time they went to the bar together.

While the group waited for their drinks, they were joined by two welcome faces. Amanda got up from her seat and hugged them both.

"Leonard, Linda," Amanda said. "You were both able to make it."

"Yes," Linda said. "We were able to find a sitter for Nate tonight."

"It's great you were able to come out," Amanda commented. "A night to honour Uncle Gerald wouldn't have been the same without the two of you."

"I believe I know everyone here," Leonard said before turning his attention to Ashley. "Except for you; I don't believe we've had the pleasure of meeting before. I'm Amanda's cousin, Leonard."

Ashley looked at Amanda and Hank, and Amanda had to stifle a giggle. Ashley extended her hand. "I'm Amanda's friend from university, Courtney," she said.

Leonard introduced his wife to Ashley, and they shook hands. Linda turned to Amanda and whispered, "I have a feeling I've met 'Courtney' before."

"You have," Amanda whispered back. "Courtney is really Ashley."

Linda's mouth fell open, aghast. "Are you serious?" she remarked. "That's Ashley from the farm? She's really dolled herself up for the night."

"The best part is the only guy of our group who knows it's her is Hank," Amanda said. "The others are all buying her story where she's studying for her Masters in Business Administration in Saskatoon."

Linda had to stifle a giggle. "That is so priceless," she said. "I can't wait to see the expression on their faces when they find out."

The waitress came by and served the original group their beverages. Leonard and Linda placed an order for a couple glasses of white wine which was served a few minutes later. Once everyone had their drinks, Leonard stood up.

He said, "We are gathered here tonight to honour the memory of a great man, my father, Amanda's uncle, and our trusted friend, Gerald Brimley. I know things haven't been easy since his passing, but he is still with us in spirit. Thanks to him, he has brought back to Saskatchewan his beloved niece, Amanda. You have all gotten to know each other for the great people you are: co-workers, and friends."

Kevin added, "And lovers." Amanda and Hank shook their heads at him with a smirk on their faces.

"Regardless of whatever our relationship is," Leonard continued, "he has brought us together and made us a stronger family. I have heard that there is someone lurking in the shadows, and they are attempting to tear us apart. However, I know as long as we stick together, we will persevere and the person who threatens us will go away. It is Gerald's will that has brought us together, and it will keep us together in the years ahead. So with that, I propose a toast to Gerald Brimley; may his warm spirit stay with us forever more."

Everyone raised their glasses and toasted. "To Gerald!" they said in unison.

Amanda stood up to speak next. "I don't think I can add much more to what Leonard has said," she stated, "but I am thankful for the opportunity to have come out to Melville, and meet all of you. Kevin, Cecil, you two might be trouble, but you're both like the brothers I never had. Thank you both for keeping me on my toes the past week."

Kevin and Cecil raised their glasses in a salute.

Amanda turned to Ashley and chose her words carefully. "Courtney," she said, "I'm so glad to have reunited with you. I feel like I've gained more than a good friend; I've gained a sister. You've been there for me during the late night chats on the phone during the past few days, and I thank you for that."

Ashley smiled and nodded to her dear friend. Amanda then focused her attention on Hank.

"Finally," she concluded, "to one Hank Acker, when I arrived at Uncle Gerald's farm last Sunday, I didn't know what to expect. I knew I would be meeting the wonderful people who worked for him. I must confess, when I first met you, I felt the same way most women do when they lay their eyes on you. However, as the days have gone on, I've gotten the opportunity to know what a warm, caring, sensitive man you are. You put my mind and heart in a tizzy, but you showed me a love and understanding any woman would desire in a man. I am thankful for your gift, and I am very honoured to have met and fallen for you."

Hank got up from his chair and gave Amanda a warm, loving hug. They exchanged a soft kiss, and he invited her to sit down in the seat beside him.

"I guess I should say something about our humble guest," he said. "Gerald has always thought of us as one big family, and I'm thankful he invited me into the fold. It was through him I was able to meet Kevin, Cecil, and Ashley. They welcomed me with open arms, and made me feel like I had a warm home. While I'm saddened over his passing, his warmth lives on. It's through that warmth he introduced Amanda into our lives. She has been a wonderful friend to us all, and has touched the heart of this weathered journeyman. I know I'm going to get flack from Kevin and Cecil for saying this, but I want everyone in our little group to hear this: I love you, Amanda Bellamy, and there's not a moment where I don't thank God for bringing you into my life."

A single tear fell from Amanda's eye. She was touched by the declaration Hank had made. She responded the only way she could. "I love you, too, Hank Acker," she said.

Leonard and Linda looked on and smiled. Ashley sighed at the happy couple, while Kevin and Cecil rolled their eyes. However, when they weren't testing their gag reflexes, the guys couldn't keep their eyes off of Ashley. To them, she was Courtney, an attractive single friend of Amanda's. They had no idea she was the same woman who has worked alongside of them the previous three years. Kevin and Cecil were transfixed by her beauty, and they were jostling each other to see who would be the first to ask her out.

"May I buy you a shooter, Courtney?" Cecil asked.

"No, Cecil," Kevin said. "I want to buy her a shooter."

"No," Cecil argued. "I am."

"Guys, guys," Ashley interrupted. "You can both buy me a shot."

"Sure thing, Courtney," Cecil said.

"What would you like?" Kevin asked.

Ashley winked at Amanda, as to say 'watch this'. She said, "How about a Blow Job?"

Kevin and Cecil were so startled by Ashley's suggestion, they almost spilled their beers. Amanda and Linda giggled at their reaction. Ashley was playing them to the hilt, and she loved every minute of it.

"Relax, guys," Ashley giggled. "I meant the shot."

Kevin and Cecil breathed a sigh of relief, and settled back into their seats; until Ashley spoke again.

She continued, "But, if either of you played your cards right..."

Hank had to hide his face, so Kevin and Cecil couldn't see him crack up over Ashley's innuendos. The guys were getting flustered over the fact this woman, who they believed they just met, was coming on to them. Kevin and Cecil excused themselves to get the shot for Ashley, and they were falling over each other en route to the bar.

184

Hank unburied his face, and said to Ashley, "You're terrible."

Ashley fluttered her eyelashes, attempting to be innocent. "Why, whatever do you mean?" she asked.

"You know what we're talking about," Amanda said. "You're stringing Kevin and Cecil along like a couple of boy toys. They might not be the sharpest knives in the drawer, but they're still part of our family."

Ashley sighed. "You're right," she resigned. "I shouldn't lead them on like this, but can't I still play with them for a little longer? I promise, if things get out of hand, I'll tell them who I *really* am."

Leonard was confused. "Wait," he said, "Courtney is not who she says she is? Who is she exactly?"

Linda patted his hand. "Look closely, dear," she said. "You'll see that she's someone you've known for a couple years now."

Leonard peered closely at the brunette, and she waved to him. It slowly started to dawn on Linda's husband. "Ashley?" he asked.

"Hi, Leonard," she said.

"You look so different than what you normally do," he commented.

"I didn't want to come out tonight in my usual attire," Ashley explained, "so I tidied myself up and slipped on a dress I had in the back of my closet."

"Well," Leonard admitted, "you certainly had me fooled."

"Had you fooled about what?" Kevin asked.

He and Cecil returned with Ashley's shot, and set it in front of her. "Sorry we took so long," Cecil said, "but we figured since we were buying Courtney a shot, we'd get one for Amanda, too."

"You didn't get me a Blow Job, too, did you?" Amanda asked.

"No," Kevin replied. "We decided to get you something a little more common, a Kamikaze."

"Do they still have that 'revenge shooter' around here?" Amanda questioned.

"The Prairie Fire," Hank said. "They do, but I don't think there's anyone in our group who we want to get back at."

"Well, no one present right now," Linda said. "I'm sure there's one certain sister-in-law of mine who would be a prime recipient of it."

"No argument from any of us here," Kevin said. "So, getting back to my original question; what did Courtney have you fooled about, Leonard?"

Leonard had to think quickly on his feet. "Oh, Courtney looked a bit like someone I knew," he said, "but obviously, she isn't."

Linda whispered to her husband, "That wasn't awkward at all."

"Sorry," he whispered back. "I had to think quickly on my feet."

Ashley and Amanda toasted each other with their shots, and knocked them back in one gulp. The guys were amazed at their gung-ho guzzling of the beverages.

"Well, that hit the spot," Ashley said.

"Would you like another?" Cecil asked.

186

"No thanks," she answered. "I'm alright for now. Maybe I'll have another one later."

"What about you, Amanda?" Kevin queried.

"I'm good, thanks," she said. "Besides, I don't want to go too overboard; I drove one of the cars here."

"That makes sense," Cecil said, "all the more for Courtney."

"Now, guys," Ashley said, "I'm not the type of girl who you expect to get drunk and take her home with you. I want to be able to save some brain cells, so I can finish my degree."

"We're sorry," Kevin said. "We didn't mean any harm by our joke."

Ashley got in a bit of a huff. "Oh, really now," she accused. "You automatically think because I'm a pretty face in a sexy dress, you think I'm the type of girl you'd like to be with?"

"No, we don't think that at all," Cecil said.

Ashley was getting pissed off. "So," she countered, "you don't think I'm the type of girl you'd like to be with?"

Hank whispered to Amanda, "Take cover; Mount Saint-Ashley's about to explode."

"We don't mean that either," Kevin said.

"Then, what is it you two clowns mean exactly?" Ashley demanded.

"Look, Courtney," Kevin explained. "Cecil and I are the type of guys who like to joke around. We say things in a light-hearted manner, but we really care about the people who mean a lot to us; like Hank, Amanda, and Ashley."

"Speaking of which," Cecil asked, "where is Ashley? Didn't she come to the bar with us tonight?"

"It was just Hank and I in my car," Amanda said.

"Linda and I drove together straight from our place," Leonard added.

Ashley smirked at Kevin and Cecil. "You two have to be the dumbest shits in the entire province," she accused. "Didn't it ever occur to you that the person you were missing was here all along?"

Kevin and Cecil looked at each other confused. They had no idea what Ashley was talking about.

Ashley let out an exasperated sigh. "Oh, for fuck sakes," she said. "Guys, it's me, Ashley."

Kevin and Cecil didn't say a word; they stood there in astonishment, with their jaws hanging open. They could not believe the woman they had been flirting with all night was the same person who slept a few doors down in the guest house.

"You're joking, right?" Cecil said.

Ashley shook her head. "Nope, 'Courtney' was me all along."

An embarrassed Kevin stammered, "Might I say you look radiant tonight?"

Ashley rolled her eyes. "It's a little too late for that," she said, "but thank you, regardless."

"Look, Ashley," Cecil said. "We didn't mean to hurt you with what we said or did. You know how we can be. If we knew it was you, we would've let up, and not try to put the moves on you."

Hank interrupted, "But, you two didn't. You drove her here tonight, and bought her a couple of drinks. It wasn't like you had her out on a dance floor, and tried to grind up against her."

"Hank's got a point there," Amanda said. "Most guys in Toronto who are trying to pick up a woman in a club almost suffocate a woman, or slip something in her drink. You two were doing a kind gesture for my friend, and being perfect gentlemen to her. Was there a slip of the tongue? Perhaps, but you two are great guys, and I'm sure if Ashley wasn't like a sister to you both, she would've been flattered you two were interested in her."

Everyone was silent as the words sunk in. Ashley's demeanor softened, and she gave Kevin and Cecil each a hug.

"I'm sorry, guys," she said. "When you two didn't recognize me back at the farm, I decided to have a little fun with it. I didn't mean for it to have gone as far as it did. I know I get on both of your cases a lot, but deep down, you two are decent men, and I'm thankful I've gotten the opportunity to know you both, and work alongside you. Leonard was right earlier when he said we've become one big family over the past three years, and I'm very fortunate to have two awesome guys I can call 'my brothers'."

"I'm very fortunate to call you 'my sister'," Kevin said.

"Me, too," Cecil added," but I have one question: if this joke continued on tonight, would you have been willing to end up in the same bed with Kevin, or me?"

Ashley gave Cecil a stern look at first, but smacked his arm and laughed. The trio shared another hug together, and the mood became more relaxed.

The rest of the evening ran smoothly with everyone consuming a couple more drinks before calling it a night. Leonard and Linda gave Amanda a hug, and told her to call them before she left for Toronto in two days time. The inhabitants of the Brimley farm made their way to their cars, and drove back to the homestead. They were careful not to go too fast, so not to rouse the suspicions of any police spot checks along their route.

~ * * * ~

The two cars arrived back at the farm without incident. Ashley, Kevin, and Cecil made their way to the guest house; however, Amanda and Hank lingered outside for a while longer.

"Thanks for everything tonight," Amanda said. "It was wonderful for all of us to get together, and let our hair down."

"You're welcome," Hank said. "I hate to imagine what would have happened had Kevin and Cecil not found out about Ashley's game. I don't think I could stand to hear her having sex with one of them."

"I don't know who would be the louder moaner of those three," Amanda mused. "I don't think Kevin or Cecil have lost their virginity yet."

Hank cringed. "Well, that's a mental cold shower in itself," he commented. "So, I guess I'll head back to the guest house for the night."

"Please, don't go," Amanda pleaded. "I was hoping you could spend the night with me tonight."

"I don't know, Amanda," Hank said. "Your mental image of Kevin or Cecil having sex was the equivalent of salt peter on me."

Amanda leaned up and kissed Hank upon his lips. He wrapped his arms around Amanda's waist and held her close. The fires of their passion began to smoulder, and Hank warmed to the idea of being in the same bed as his lover. Amanda took Hank's hand in hers and led him up the porch steps. She was about to open the front door when she saw the legal notice affixed to the structure, and her heart sank in an instant. Rebecca Brimley had finally made her move.

CHAPTER TWENTY-ONE

Kevin, Cecil, and Ashley ran out of the guest house when they heard Amanda yell 'Fuck!' The heir uttered the profanity so loud all of Saskatchewan could have heard her. The farmhands' worst fear had come to fruition when they read the note Amanda held in her hands. They all agreed it was a heinous act for Rebecca to send her lawyer to the homestead while everyone was out toasting Gerald. If there was one good thing that came out of it, they were thankful the Summons wasn't served in front of everyone at the bar; the lawyer would not have made it out of the establishment alive.

"Damn that bitch," Ashley fumed. "She's got a lot of nerve to dredge this up, just as Amanda is about to leave for home."

"We feared this was going to happen," Hank said. "Rebecca knew Amanda was leaving in a couple days, and she wanted to file the papers now in hopes Amanda wouldn't get any more time off of work to state her case."

"It was all a calculated ploy on her part," Kevin added. "Rebecca knows it's her word against ours, and without Gerald's main defendant present, this farm is as good as hers."

"You know we all have Gerald's and your backs, Amanda," Cecil said.

"Thanks, Cecil," Amanda said. "I'm appreciative of all of your support. However, if Rebecca thinks I'm going to let her steamroll her way in and steal this place away from all of us, she has another thing coming. This farm is *our* home, and I'll be damned if I let that vindictive bitch take it away from us."

Amanda's adopted family hugged their pseudo-sister. Everyone vowed they would take Rebecca head on in the courts. They would attempt to establish Gerald Brimley's character as outstanding; taking the motley crew of three men and one woman from different parts of the Prairies into his home, and became a father figure to them all. Through him, they became more than co-workers on a humble corn farm on the outskirts of Melville, Saskatchewan; they became a family. Yes, they had their own relatives via their blood; however, in this little hamlet in the Canadian West, the stars had aligned to bring these five friends together to forge a union that would last a lifetime.

Hank suggested they all try to get some sleep, but Amanda was still fuming. He agreed to keep her company while she simmered down. Their plans to rekindle the magic from earlier in the day had been squelched, but Amanda and Hank hoped the time together would help solidify their relationship.

~ * * * ~

The couple moved to the den where Hank was sitting on the loveseat while Amanda paced back and forth. She was still upset, and her lover attempted to soothe her with some reassuring words.

"That selfish, self-centered, egotistical slut," Amanda said. "I should have known she was going to screw us over just before I left."

"Technically," Hank said, "we had a feeling this was going to be her ploy all along, remember?"

Amanda shot a glare at Hank. "I know we figured she would," she said. "I didn't think she would stoop so low as to have served the papers while we were out honouring my uncle."

"Rebecca was never really fond of this place to begin with," Hank explained. "She had been trying to get Gerald to sell it for years. When he wouldn't budge, she wasn't all that impressed; calling her father stubborn and pig-headed. That's why she relished his passing. She automatically believed she would receive the farm in the Will. That way, she could sell the farm and reap all of the profits for herself. However, Gerald knew me and the others would have lost our home, and be out of a job if she got it. So, he bequeathed it to someone he loved and trusted."

Amanda rubbed her arms. "I'm thankful he did," she said. "If it wasn't for him, I wouldn't have met any of his crew; especially the man I've fallen head over heels for."

Hank stood up, walked over to Amanda, and wrapped his arms around her. "Nor would I have had the opportunity to meet the most beautiful woman I have ever known," he said. "I consider the past week to have been a blessing because I've been able to find the woman I want to spend my time with."

Amanda blushed. "Thanks, Hank," she replied. "The feeling is mutual."

A sly grin emerged on Hank's face. "You've been able to find the woman of your dreams, too?" he asked.

Amanda laughed and smacked Hank's arm. Then, she hugged him, nestling her head against his chest; hearing his heart beat through his shirt. She let out a contented sigh as he kissed her forehead, and ran his fingers through her long auburn locks. Amanda looked up at her lover, gazing into his eyes. Hank smiled down at her; then, brought his lips to hers for a soft, tender kiss.

"I could stay in your arms all night," she said.

"We could, if you wanted," he replied.

"I'm not in the mood for sex tonight, Hank," Amanda said. "Not after reading the Summons."

"Now, Amanda," Hank said, "you know I'm not all about that. We can just lie on your bed, in each other's arms. No hanky-panky; just me holding you, and making you feel safe and secure."

Amanda sighed again. "What did I ever do to deserve such a warm, caring man like you?" she asked.

"You were born as the niece of Gerald Brimley," he noted. "It's thanks to him we were brought together, and I am forever grateful for it."

The two retired to Amanda's room, and true to his word, Hank and Amanda slept together with their clothes on. They wrapped their arms around each other, listening to each other's breath, and whispering terms of endearment until they drifted off; happy, content, and in love with one another.

~ * * * ~

The sun rose the next morning, and shone through the curtains hanging in Amanda's window. Amanda began to stir in her bed, and at the same time, Hank awoke from his slumber. The two of them smiled at each other, as they recognized each other's faces.

"Morning, babe," he said.

"Morning, sweetie," she responded.

The two of them shared a kiss, and Amanda grimaced. "Ugh," she said, "you have some nasty morning breath."

Hank chuckled. "So do you," he replied, "but I blame that on all the booze we drank last night."

"You're probably right," Amanda said. "Do you mind if I go brush my teeth?"

Hank released Amanda from his grasp. "Not at all," he said. "Can I borrow some of your mouthwash when you're done?"

Amanda scurried to the bathroom. "Sure thing, dear," she said.

Hank stretched out on the bed while Amanda freshened up. Her head was throbbing a bit from the mild hangover she was suffering. She didn't think she had that much to drink, but it appeared she couldn't hold as much alcohol in her system as she did in her university days. The years had made her more susceptible to the toxin.

"I hope the others were able to get a decent night's sleep," Hank said.

"I just hope Ashley's not as buzzed as I'm feeling right now," Amanda said. "There must've been some extra booze in that shot Cecil gave me."

"That's something you'll have to ask him about," he said, "but you and Ashley did knock those back pretty quickly."

"I didn't want to come across like a prissy little thing," she reasoned. "I may be more responsible when I'm at the office in Toronto, but there's still a gal who grew up on the Prairies in me."

"Did you have fun last night?" Hank asked.

"I had an amazing time until we got back," Amanda replied. "Of course, who wouldn't be upset over such a buzz kill?"

"You should call Leonard and give him the heads up about the little surprise left on the door," he suggested.

"I'll give him a call after breakfast," Amanda said, as was finishing in the bathroom. The heir walked over to Hank. "It's your turn, now," she commented.

Hank rolled off the bed, and headed off to rinse his mouth out. As he passed Amanda, she smacked him on his ass.

"Someone's in the mood this morning," he said.

"Since we didn't do anything last night," she explained, "I guess my hormones are still in overdrive."

"Are you sure we should be doing that with the way we're feeling?" Hank asked.

Amanda grinned. "They do say sex can help cure certain headaches," she said.

"Those are for migraines," he noted. "I doubt they'd be effective for hangovers."

"I'm more than willing to put that theory to the test," she stated.

Hank spit out his oral rinse, and dried his mouth. "As tempting as that may be," he responded, "I think it'd be better to get something in our stomachs first."

Amanda smiled at her lover. "I'd rather have a nice breakfast sausage in my mouth," she said.

Hank laughed. "You're terrible," he said.

"I can't help it," Amanda defended. "I'm a kitten, and having you near me makes me purr."

Hank walked over to Amanda, and gave her a kiss. "That's much better," he said.

"I agree," she said, "now about your smoked link."

Hank chuckled. "Will you stop already?" he said.

Amanda pouted. "I don't like this Hank," she complained. "Where's the one I made love to yesterday morning?"

"He still there," Hank reassured, "but he can't function without a full stomach."

Amanda sighed. "Fine," she said, "we'll get something to eat first, but you owe me, mister."

Hank kissed her again. "I promise I'll pay you back," he said, "and with interest."

Hank headed downstairs, and Amanda used the opportunity to change out of her outfit from the night before. She was hoping she could have ridden him in her slip-dress, but her dream didn't come to fruition. It would have to wait for another time.

~ * * * ~

Amanda slipped on her jeans and a cotton shirt before heading to the dining room. When she arrived, she found Ashley sitting at the table, looking a little worse for wear, while she sipped on a cup of homemade coffee. Kevin and Cecil fared no better, but they were still coherent enough to fry up some bacon and eggs.

"Looks like you guys are paying for last night too, huh?" Amanda said.

"That's the last time I talk myself into having a shot." Ashley said.

"They were rather potent suckers," Amanda noted.

Ashley asked Kevin, "You guys didn't tell the bartender to make them doubles, did you?"

"We might have told him to make them extra strong," he said.

Ashley rubbed her forehead in a bid to relieve the throbbing pain. "So help me God, you two," she threatened. "Once I recover from this, I'm so going to kick both your asses."

Hank stepped in. "Easy there, Ashley," he said. "We're all paying for our overindulgence last night, but the main thing is we all went out and had fun."

Cecil said, "Easy for you to say; you had Amanda to curl up next to last night."

"I had to calm her down," Hank explained. "She was still pretty upset about receiving the Summons."

"I still am," Amanda said, "but I'm going to call Leonard, and tell him to get in touch with Mr. Mitchell. I don't know if he'll be able to get him on a Saturday, but we need to prepare our case. Rebecca had this planned all along, so she could catch us when we were the least prepared. If we can prove to the court that Gerald had all of his faculties, we can make sure we'll be able to keep the farm."

"I hope so," Kevin said. "I don't want to have to look elsewhere for a job. I like it here."

"We all like it here," Ashley said. "I'll be damned if we get split up."

Cecil and Kevin brought in the bacon and eggs, and everyone dug in. The greasy meal was exactly what everyone needed; it helped lessen the lingering effects from the night before. While the coffee wasn't the Timmy's everyone had grown accustomed to every morning, it still hit the spot, and helped wake them up.

Amanda looked around the table, and sighed. She was going to miss these meals together. They had become a ritual; the camaraderie with her adopted family. Forty-eight hours from this moment, she would be back in Toronto, having breakfast alone. There would be no conversations at the table, no joking between the boys and Ashley, and most importantly, no Hank to look at from across the table. She was going to miss his smiling face the most of all. Amanda wished she could pack all of them in her suitcase, and take them with her back to Toronto. Alas, such a wish could never come true. Instead, she vowed to enjoy as much of her last day with them as she could.

"You know, Ashley," Amanda said, "it's been years since I've seen how the corn gets collected and processed. Is there any way you could show me how the Processing Machine works?"

"The corn crop hasn't started growing yet," she said. "Why would you..." Ashley looked at Amanda, and saw the heir's need to bond one more time. "Sure," Ashley replied. "I'll show you after breakfast."

Amanda smiled. "Thank you," she said. "Just give me a chance to call Leonard first." Amanda turned her attention to Kevin and Cecil. "And guys," she asked, "could you take me out into the fields after lunch and let me watch you guys work?"

Not one to miss the sentiment, Cecil said, "We can do that, Amanda. Not a problem at all."

"I'm surprised you haven't decided to come out there with us already," Kevin said.

"I was reluctant since the crop just got into the ground," she said, "but I remember coming out here as a kid during my summers, and playing in the rows of corn stalks. I know it won't be the same, but I want to go out there and remember all of the fun times I had."

"Anything to help recapture your youth," Kevin said.

Amanda smiled. "Thanks, guys," she replied. "I truly appreciate it."

The rest of the day went on as scheduled. Leonard told Amanda he would get in touch with Gerald's lawyer, and if he heard anything back from Mr. Mitchell, he'd let her know. Afterwards, Ashley showed her the workings of the Processor; then later, the guys took Amanda out into the fields. She walked along the rows of this year's crop. The seedlings had yet to sprout, but Amanda closed her eyes and envisioned running amongst the growing stalks. She realized there was no other place she'd rather be. Yes, she would be leaving for Toronto the next day, but to her, this farm would always be her home, and Rebecca Brimley would never take that away from her.

CHAPTER TWENTY-TWO

A spring rain fell on Highway 10. It was a sad day for everyone on the Brimley farm; the young woman who had spent the past couple of weeks amongst them was leaving to head back to her regular job back east. Kevin and Cecil wanted to make the journey to the airport in Regina, but Ashley thought it was best if they stayed behind, in the event Rebecca tried any further funny business. Ashley sat in the passenger seat beside Leonard, while Amanda and Hank held hands and cuddled in the backseat. It would be the last moments the two lovers would have together until she returned. The only problem was no one knew if she would have anything to return to.

Leonard figured Mr. Mitchell would be able to continue work on Gerald's case Monday morning. However, everyone was still on pins and needles regarding the case. Rebecca's lawyer alleged he had proof of her father's mental incapacities, but they still needed to be displayed in a court of law. While Leonard, Amanda, and everyone on the farm disputed the claims, they knew their day before the judge would be approaching soon.

The main stickler for Gerald's case was Amanda. Since the farm was originally bequeathed to her, she would need to be present in order to strengthen Gerald's defense. The only problem was, after a week away from her Advertising Executive job, Amanda didn't know if she would be granted any more time off for the trial. Everyone feared they would lose the case if Amanda wasn't in attendance for the proceedings. She needed to be there, but would she show up?

"I'm sorry you have to leave before everything's been taken care of," Ashley said.

"I am, too," Amanda replied. "But, I will do everything in my power to make it back for the legal proceedings."

"It would be great if you could," Leonard said. "It will show we have a united front, and will strengthen the case for Dad."

"It depends on what Mr. Lawrence says back at the office," Amanda said. "He was alright with me taking two weeks off to get over Uncle Gerald's passing, but he might not be as forthcoming when he finds out I have to come back for the trial."

"You think he's going to force you to pick what's more important?" Hank asked.

"It is a concern," she replied. "Do I choose to stay at my advertising job in Toronto and lose the farm, or do I come back to Melville and give up everything I've worked for the past few years?"

Ashley asked, "If it came to that, do you have any idea what you'd choose?"

Amanda sighed. "I don't know," she said. "I'm hoping it doesn't come to that, but in the event it does, I have to look inside myself, and decide what is best for me."

There was a look of concern from everyone in the car. They hoped Amanda would come to bat for them, but would she be willing to risk her career for it? She had worked so hard to establish herself in Toronto; her job was all she dreamed of. That was until fate brought her back home to Saskatchewan. She forged many friendships with the people who worked for her uncle, and even begun a relationship with the man of her dreams. Would she be willing to give up her business job for the simple life on the farm? It was a decision that played on her mind, but she tried to push it to the back recesses of it. She had to resume her normal life; however, the past week would have to be recalled instantly when she received the call from Leonard. It was a situation she knew would come, and a decision she knew she'd be forced to make.

Before Amanda walked through security to catch her flight, everyone said their goodbyes to her. Leonard reassured her he would be in touch. Ashley gave her pseudo-sister a big hug, and told her to look inside her heart. She would know what to decide when the time came. The longest goodbye was saved for Hank.

"I guess this is so long for now," he said.

"Don't worry, honey," Amanda said. "I will do my best to be here for the trial. I won't let you guys down."

"I'll be waiting for you to return," Hank said. "I'll write you an email every chance I get; provided Kevin and Cecil aren't hogging the computer."

Amanda gave a weak smile while choking back her tears. "I'd like that," she said. "I know it's not the same as a phone call, but it'll be less expensive in the long run."

Hank's sadness began to creep onto his face. "I'm going to miss you, babe," he said.

"I'll miss you too, Hank," she replied.

The couple embraced and gave each other a long, deep kiss. It would have lasted forever, but Amanda broke away from Hank's lips, and said she needed to catch her flight. She waved to the three one more time before she zipped through the security doors.

Amanda found her seat on the plane, and looked out the window at the terminal building. As the plane pulled away from the gate, tears began to fall from her eyes. She was going to miss everyone at the farm: Kevin, Cecil, Ashley, and especially, Hank. However, she knew if she was going to keep all of them together, she needed to come back for the trial. It was the only solution she had.

~ * * * ~

Amanda settled back into her advertising job, and things were hectic, as per usual. The stack of files for the projects she worked on was as tall as when she left for Melville, if not taller. Whenever she got a free moment, her mind would drift off to the time she recently spent on her uncle's farm. She remembered back to the easy pace life had been; the relationships she formed with the people who helped keep it afloat after Gerald's passing, and the whirlwind romance she shared with the journeyman who touched her soul.

She had kept in contact with Hank over the days since her return. He'd inform her of how Kevin and Cecil were still up to their old tricks, and Ashley would constantly admonish them for it. Life had returned to a relative normal on the farm; however, everyone missed Amanda, and they wished she would come back soon. The sentiment touched Amanda, and she wrote about missing all of them, too. Hank and Amanda would share some romantic words for each other, but it wasn't the same. She missed being held in his arms, his warm kisses, and lying in the same bed with him. It didn't appear she would return anytime soon, until a fortnight after she started back to work. It was when she received the call from Leonard.

206

The trial was slated a week from then, and they needed Amanda to be there to give her testimony. Without it, and the farm was as good as Rebecca's. The staff would lose their home and their jobs, and Rebecca would laugh all the way to the bank; crowing about how she had finally won the war. Amanda was determined not to let that happen. Gerald Brimley meant a lot to everyone she knew in Melville, and she would be damned if his daughter stole everyone's livelihood away from them.

As soon as the call ended, Amanda rushed to Mr. Lawrence's office. He was busy looking over the latest project she had submitted when she knocked on his door.

"Mr. Lawrence," she asked, "may I have a word with you, please?"

"What is it, Amanda?" he said.

"I've just received a call from my cousin Leonard," Amanda explained. "I've been called to testify in a civil suit regarding my Uncle Gerald's farm."

"Is there something wrong?" Mr. Lawrence asked.

"My cousin Rebecca is contesting his Will," she stated. "She's claiming my inheritance should go to her. I have to be back in Regina for next Monday to state my case."

Mr. Lawrence removed his glasses, and rubbed his eyes. "I don't think I can allow you to leave for the proceedings," he said.

"May I inquire why, sir?" Amanda asked.

"You were just there two weeks ago to help grieve your uncle's passing," Mr Lawrence explained. "I know you worked on the Palmerton account while you were out there, but what you submitted was unsatisfactory."

"I apologize, Mr. Lawrence," she said. "I worked on it as much as I could."

"I appreciate the effort," he replied, "but I feel if you're going to be an effective advertising executive, you need to be here in the office; not out in the middle of nowhere, being distracted by some corn field."

"I'm sorry you feel that way, sir. But, if I'm not present to give my testimony, my inheritance will revert directly to Rebecca."

"Miss Bellamy," Mr. Lawrence stated, "I understand you want to protect your interests, but I feel you're needed more here in the office. Now, if you want to go out to Regina to testify, then I believe you're not the right fit for this company."

Amanda blinked. "Are you asking me to choose between my inheritance and my job?" she asked.

"I don't want to phrase it like that," he answered, "but yes; that's what it boils down to."

Amanda thought about the ultimatum Mr. Lawrence gave her. Within seconds she gave her response. "I'll clear out my desk," she said. "It's been a pleasure working for you."

CHAPTER TWENTY-THREE

There was an eerie calm in the courtroom. A few people from Melville had filed into the gallery to hear the upcoming civil case between Gerald's estate and Rebecca. Kevin, Cecil, Ashley, and Hank sat in the first row behind Mr. Mitchell, and they waited for the start of the proceedings.

"Do you think she'll come?" Kevin asked.

"I tried to get a hold of her," Hank said, "but, she hasn't been answering her email the past couple of days."

"That's not a good sign," Cecil said. "Without Amanda here, we're going to lose the farm for sure."

"Take it easy, guys," Ashley said. "I'm sure she will be here. She's probably held up in traffic."

A couple of moments later, Rebecca strutted into the courtroom. She had a smug demeanor to her; dressed in a dark blue power suit with a red camisole. She stopped before the foursome and began clucking at them.

"At least there are some supporters here from Daddy's farm," Rebecca crowed. "I was afraid this was going to be more of a cakewalk than it already is."

"You haven't won yet, Rebecca," Ashley said. "The farm is still in Amanda's possession."

"It's funny you should say that because I don't see her present with you," Rebecca said.

"She's probably on her way as we speak," Hank said.

A smirk emerged on Rebecca's face. "Aw, that's so nice of you to stick up for your girlfriend," she said, "but I find her absence disturbing. Face it; she's a Toronto girl now. She moved away from here for a reason, and you think she's going to come back to defend what you folks hold dear? Give me a break. The farm is going to come to someone who truly deserves it; someone who still lives in Saskatchewan. But, don't worry, Hank. I'm sure after I've sold the place, I can hire you on as my boy toy, and you and I can spend our nights together cuddling underneath the stars."

Hank gave Gerald's daughter a cold stare. "I'd rather live my days back in the Oil Sands," he replied.

"Suit yourself," Rebecca said, "but remember, Hank, you're going to need a place to live after the farm's sold. The offer is still on the table."

Rebecca took her seat at the opposing desk with her attorney, and basked in her confidence. The staff hated her with a passion, but she was right. Unless Amanda arrived soon, their case wouldn't have a leg to stand on. Ashley lowered her head and said a prayer; hoping her pseudo-sister would show up right away.

The bailiff announced for everyone to rise for the presence of the judge, the Honourable Martin T. Shellbrook. Once he took his seat, everyone sat back down.

"We are here today to hear the case of Rebecca Brimley vs. The Estate of Gerald Brimley," he announced.

A couple seconds after, the doors to the courtroom opened, and in walked Mr. Mitchell, Leonard, and Amanda. Amanda was dressed in a green blazer, white camisole, and a black pencil skirt.

"So glad of you to finally show up for the proceedings, Mr. Mitchell," Judge Shellbrook said.

"My apologies, your honour," Mr. Mitchell replied. "The traffic outside of the courthouse was a nightmare."

"I entrust you are prepared for the case you're defending?" the magistrate asked.

"Yes, your honour," the lawyer replied.

The judge turned his attention to Rebecca's attorney. "The counsel of the plaintiff may begin his opening remarks," he said.

Amanda turned to the gang sitting behind her and whispered, "I bet you guys thought you'd never see me again, huh?"

Cecil said, "To say we weren't worried about you showing up for this would be a lie."

Hank said, "When I hadn't heard back from you for a couple of days, I thought something was wrong."

"Yeah, about that," Amanda said, "there have been some drastic changes going on lately, and I've been occupied with those."

"What kind of changes," Ashley asked.

"I'll explain after the proceedings," said the heir.

The courtroom heard the statements from both Rebecca's attorney and Mr. Mitchell. They stated their cases trying to establish the mental capacities of Gerald in a bid to determine if his Will was valid, or if it should be struck down. Amanda looked at Leonard and saw he was worried about Rebecca's challenge. Should the Will be declared void, it would put the investments he received for his inheritance in jeopardy. The nest egg he and Linda were establishing for Nathan's college fund would be no more; save for what little was in it before the inheritance.

Leonard, Amanda, and the staff all made their case on Gerald's behalf; stating he was a warm, caring individual who was beloved by everyone who came into contact with him. Rebecca was the only person to dispute their claims; citing he was a stubborn person who put others before his own family. The proceedings were devolving into a character assassination on Rebecca's part; making her more loathed than she already was. After the closing statements, Judge Shellbrook retired to his chamber where he would contemplate the evidence before him, and return with his verdict.

"I think we might have this one," Mr. Mitchell told Amanda and the others.

"Are you sure about that," Amanda asked. "Rebecca's attorney was doing her best to drag Uncle Gerald's name through the mud."

"Miss Brimley didn't win many people over with her accusations," he explained. "I believe since it was all of us bestowing the virtues and character of him, it helped paint a clearer picture of what type of man he was."

"I hope you're right, Mr. Mitchell," Ashley said. "I don't want us to lose our homes and livelihood because of Rebecca's bitterness towards her father."

"I know you don't," Mr. Mitchell said. "However, the case is now in Judge Shellbrook's hands. Personally, if I was the one presiding over things, I'd award it in Gerald's favour, but that's just me. It depends on how he interprets all the findings."

Hank took Amanda's hands in his. "I know you were going to tell me after the verdict," he said, "but I have to know about these changes you were talking about earlier."

"It's a long story, Hank," she said, "but the short version is, I'm no longer at my advertising executive job."

Everyone looked at Amanda aghast. "Wait," Hank asked, "they fired you because you had to leave to come to the trial?"

Amanda was about to explain when Judge Shellbrook came back to the Bench.

"I have weighed all of the evidence from both parties in this matter," he stated. "While Miss Brimley raised the point where she believes she is entitled to Gerald Brimley's property in Melville based on the premise of her lineage, she has gone about it in a bid to discredit the man who raised her during her formative years. We heard testimony today from other members of Gerald Brimley's family and his colleagues to dispute the plaintiff's accusations. They established that Gerald Brimley was a good man who cared about those who mattered to him the most. Through her testimony, it was made clear the plaintiff didn't feel he shared the same warmth and kindness to her. Her claim was made out of spite and hatred. That is why I rule in the favour of The Estate of Gerald Brimley, and declare him to have been of sound mind; ergo, his Last Will and Testament is to be deemed valid. Case dismissed."

Judge Shellbrook banged his gavel to make his decision final. Amanda and the others hugged each other while Rebecca fumed over the decision and stormed out of the courtroom; glaring at them as she passed.

"We did it," Kevin said. "We still have the farm."

"Thank you for all of your help, Mr. Mitchell," Amanda told her attorney.

"It was my pleasure, Miss Bellamy," he said. "I know how much Gerald meant to all of you, and I wanted to make sure you didn't lose the precious gifts he gave all of you."

"Is there any way we can repay you for all of your hard work?" Ashley asked.

"There's no repayment necessary," Mr. Mitchell said. "However, if you are insistent on doing so, might I suggest that you make a donation to the Canadian Cancer Society. Gerald made sure to donate to them on an annual basis, and if you wouldn't mind carrying on that tradition in his name, it would be greatly appreciated."

"We'll make sure to do that, Mr. Mitchell," Leonard said. "Thank you again for all of your help."

"You're welcome, Leonard," the lawyer replied. Mr. Mitchell grabbed his briefcase and left the courtroom. The others lingered in the gallery and allowed the verdict to sink in. The farm Hank, Ashley, Kevin, and Cecil called home was still in Amanda's name, and she would allow them to continue to work and live on the quaint property on the outskirts of Melville.

Hank took Amanda's hands in his. "So, if I heard you right," he said, "you said you're no longer working for your advertising firm in Toronto?"

"That's right," Amanda said.

"I'm so sorry to hear that, sweetie," Ashley said. "Did they fire you because of the court date?"

"They didn't fire me because of it," Amanda said. "I quit."

"Hold on a second," Kevin said. "You quit a cushy job in the big city just to fight for us?"

Amanda nodded. "Yes," she said, "I did."

"Isn't that a little off to do that," Cecil asked.

"One might think that," Amanda explained, "but over the past couple of weeks, I've had time to evaluate what things mean the most to me: my family, my friends, and my loved ones."

"So, now that you're out of a job," Kevin asked, "what are you going to do now?"

Amanda smiled. "Well, there is this nice little place out in Melville that I've grown quite fond of," she said.

"Does this mean what I think it means," Leonard asked.

Amanda interlaced her fingers with Hank's. "Yes, it does, Leonard," she said. "I'm moving back to Saskatchewan; I'm coming home."

CHAPTER TWENTY-FOUR

It was a bright, sunny afternoon on the farm in Melville. Over a year had passed since the verdict granting Gerald Brimley's farm to his niece was rendered. Amanda had readjusted to life on the Prairies after living in Toronto for the five years after she graduated from university in Saskatoon. However, after the two weeks she had spent on the farm in the days after her uncle's passing, she knew this was where she truly belonged. She was able to reconnect with the places and people who meant the most to her. She was afraid the people of Melville would shun her as someone who had abandoned her home to live a supposed better life in the big city. However, since moving back to Saskatchewan, she began to win everyone over. The town welcomed her back with open arms, and she was grateful for it. Of course, having people like Kevin, Cecil, Ashley, and Hank to expedite the process helped, as well.

Leonard knocked on Amanda's door. "Are you almost ready in there?" he asked. "We're about ready to start."

"Just keep your shirt on," Ashley said. "You can't mess with perfection."

"Alright, but please hurry up," he said. "We don't want to keep the guests waiting."

"They've waited for as long as they have, Leonard," she stated. "A few more minutes isn't going to kill them."

Amanda said to Ashley, "Thank you for helping me get ready for this."

"Anytime, sweetie," Ashley replied. "You would've done the same for me. And, thank you for making me your maid of honour."

"It's the least I could have done," Amanda said. "You've been a sister to me ever since I first arrived here back in April of last year, and I wanted you to be a part of my special day. If it wasn't for you, I wouldn't be here right now."

Ashley said, "I knew back then the two of you were perfect for each other, and now here you are; getting ready to walk down the aisle and proclaim yourselves to each other forever. Truthfully, it's as special a day for all of us, as much as it's yours. I'm just thankful to be part of it."

Amanda took Ashley's hand in hers. "Ashley," she explained, "we may have been born to separate parents, but Uncle Gerald brought all of us together, and made us a family. I am honoured to have you as part of mine."

The two women hugged one another, but were careful not to mess up each other's gowns.

"Are you ready for your big moment?" Ashley asked.

Amanda smiled. "I've been waiting a year for this," she said. "It's time."

~ * * * ~

Ashley and Amanda exited the bedroom, and made their way downstairs. Once they arrived, they grabbed their respective bouquets, and took their positions. Amanda peered out the window

217

and saw half the town had assembled in the rows of chairs which had been set up. She saw the top part of the erected altar, and caught a brief glimpse of Hank standing next to the reverend. The look was too quick to recognize him all dressed up, but Amanda knew in a few moments she would be standing beside him; ready to declare her desire to spend the rest of her life with him.

A solemn hymn started playing and the wedding procession made their way down the aisle. First, little Nathan walked down; carrying a pillow that held the rings. Next was Ashley, who marched down the aisle, and took her spot off to the side. Finally, the organist started playing "Here Comes the Bride", and Amanda appeared at the doorway. She was dressed in a cream-coloured sequined gown; a white veil covered her face. By her side was Leonard to lead her down the aisle.

As Amanda proceeded to the altar, she passed by a sea of smiling faces of fellow townsfolk who were happy for her. She was becoming one of them, and agreed to spend the rest of her days in Melville. The whole time she and Leonard marched, her eyes were transfixed at the people who stood at the altar. To her left was Ashley in a pink gown, and to her right were Kevin and Cecil in designer tuxedos. There was a dispute over who would be the best man for the ceremony. However, not wanting to cause any jealousy between the two, Hank and Amanda agreed they would co-host the position. Then, her eyes met the man she'd been waiting to see.

Hank was dressed in a black tuxedo, and looked more gorgeous than he normally did. He had shaved off his notorious stubble for the occasion, and it brought out a youthful look to him. Amanda giggled at the thought of this being the last few moments anyone would see him as the most eligible single man in the Prairies. She had caught the biggest fish in the pond, and Amanda wasn't going to let him go for anything.

Amanda and Leonard arrived at the altar. The two shared a hug, and Leonard took his seat. Hank lifted her veil, and he was once again struck by her beauty. The reverend opened his Bible and began the ceremony.

"Dearly beloved," he spoke, "we are gathered here today to witness the holy union between Amanda and Hank."

The reverend continued his spiel with the usual Bible verse recitals. Amanda and Hank held each other's hands and smiled at each other. It was hard to believe that these two people, who had met over a year prior, would be together underneath the blue Saskatchewan sky, declaring themselves to one another. It was the happiest day in both of their lives, and it couldn't have been more perfect.

"I believe Amanda and Hank have written their own vows," the reverend said. "Hank, would you care to go first?"

Hank pulled out his prepared speech from his suit pocket, and began to read.

"Amanda," he said, "they say true love happens for a reason. I never knew what that reason was until I first met you. You brought a warmth and understanding I have never encountered before in my life. You are the ray of prairie sun that brightens up my day, and I thank Gerald, with an assist from the Good Lord above, for bringing you back home and into my life."

"Thank you, Hank," the reverend said. "Amanda, it's your turn."

Amanda didn't fumble around for any prepared speech cards; she looked into Hank's eyes and spoke.

"Hank," she said, "when I first arrived on this farm all of those months ago, I was a scared woman. I had just inherited this farm, and I didn't know what to expect. It was on that rainy Sunday I was blessed to have met the members of our wedding party. But most importantly, I met the man standing here before me today. I think back to that day, and I remember being caught by how attractive you were on the outside. However, as the days progressed, I began to see how attractive you were on the inside, as well. You showed me warmth, honesty, kindness, and love. It's those qualities I admire the most, and it is why I vow to spend the rest of my life with you."

The reverend said, "Thank you, Amanda, for those touching words. I know this will not be a popular question to ask, but it is a common tradition. If there is anyone who objects to these two getting married, speak now or forever hold your peace."

Silence emanated from the crowd, as no one spoke. This was made evident when Ashley shot a daring glare at the audience. She wasn't going to let anyone spoil Hank and Amanda's special day.

The reverend continued, "Now, it is time for the all important question. Henry James, do you take Amanda Patricia to be your lawfully wedded spouse, to have and to hold, in sickness and in health, for as long as you both shall live?"

Hank looked into Amanda's eyes and said, "I do." Kevin took the ring from Nate's pillow, handed it to the groom, and Hank slipped the ring on Amanda's finger.

"Amanda Patricia," the reverend asked, "do you take Henry James to be your lawfully wedded spouse, to have and to hold, in sickness and in health, for as long as you both shall live?"

Amanda looked back at Hank, smiled at him, and nodded. "Yes," she said, "I do."

Ashley procured the ring from Nate's pillow, handed it to Amanda, who slipped it onto her new husband's finger.

The reverend said, "Then, with the power invested in me, and the province of Saskatchewan, I declare you both husband and wife. Ladies and gentlemen, I present to you, Mr. and Mrs. Henry James Acker. You may now kiss each other."

Hank and Amanda embraced each other and shared their first kiss as a married couple. The crowd assembled rose to their feet and applauded the happy couple. Amanda hugged the others in the wedding party, and Hank shook the hands of the reverend, his best men, and Leonard. Everyone else shuffled off to another section of the estate where the wedding reception took place.

~ * * * ~

The banquet was an extravagant affair with regional delicacies offered to the guests. It would have made sense to have held it in a licensed hall, but with the weather holding up, and a big tent erected, it was enough to accommodate the four hundred people who assembled for the festivities. Everyone came by and offered their congratulations to the happy couple. Amongst them happened to be Mr. Mitchell, the attorney who handled Gerald's affairs.

Hank shook Mr. Mitchell's hand. "Mr. Mitchell," he said, "we're so glad you were able to make it."

"Thank you," the lawyer said. "Congratulations to you both; it was a lovely ceremony. I just wanted to ask if your cousin has caused you any more trouble in recent days."

"Rebecca wouldn't have dared to show up for the wedding," Amanda said. "Thankfully, we haven't heard from her in months. She probably crawled back under her rock ever since the verdict was handed down last year."

"That must be a relief to you both," Mr. Mitchell said.

"It is," Amanda said, "and I'm thankful she's not here. Her presence would have ruined our special day, and I don't think the wedding party would have appreciated it."

The lawyer laughed. "Yes, I saw the 'death stare' Ashley gave everyone when the reverend asked if anyone had any objections to your union," he said. "If Miss Brimley was here and spoke up at that point, those two would have gone at it on the spot."

Hank chuckled. "It would have made for some interesting entertainment, to say the least," he remarked.

"Anyway," Mr. Mitchell said, "I just wanted to come by and congratulate you both on your nuptials; may your marriage be long and prosperous."

"Thank you, Mr. Mitchell," Hank replied.

~ * * * ~

After everyone dined on the wedding dinner, Amanda and Hank took to the dance floor for the ceremonial first dance. Many wondered what song they would pick for the occasion, but everyone was relieved when they picked a country ballad sung by a male artist from Alberta. The couple shared another kiss, and swayed to the music. Amanda rested her head on Hank's chest as they danced; content for their special moment together.

"I love you, Mr. Acker," Amanda said.

"I love you, too, Mrs. Acker," Hank said. "I'm surprised you didn't decide to hyphenate your name."

"I thought about it," she reasoned, "but Mrs. Acker-Bellamy sounded too long. I'm content with being Mrs. Hank Acker."

"It's a shame you had to give up your job in Toronto to come back to Melville," he said.

"It was," Amanda explained, "but it's given me a chance to freelance for some budding firms in Regina. Besides, life in Toronto was becoming far too hectic. I prefer a simpler pace, and a freedom to work on the things I want, instead of being forced to work long hours. Here, I can dictate my own work day, and still spend time on the things and people who are the most important to me."

"I hope Kevin and Cecil won't give us any trouble now that we're husband and wife," Hank said.

Amanda said, "Hank, sweetie, this is Kevin and Cecil we're talking about here. You know that if there's trouble around, those two are bound to find it."

Hank laughed. "You got a point there," he said. "Thankfully, Ashley is still around to help keep those two in line."

"Do you ever think Ashley will find someone to make her as happy as you make me?" she asked.

"That's hard to say," he said. "I don't know if there's another one of me around."

Amanda smacked Hank's arm in jest. "You know what I mean," she said.

Hank smiled. "I do," he said, "and honestly, I'm not sure, but if there's anyone else who deserves to have a special someone in her life, it's Ashley."

~ * * * ~

Once the first dance was over, Amanda announced it was time to throw her bouquet. A crowd of single women in attendance gathered on the dance floor. Amanda turned her back to them, and tossed her bouquet over her shoulder. All of the women jostled for the sailing bouquet, but the arrangement would find its way into the hands of the maid of honour.

"Congratulation, Ashley," Amanda yelled.

"That was sheer luck," Ashley laughed. "I doubt that prophecy will come true."

"Well, there is still the male equivalent to this," Hank said. "Amanda, honey, would you mind taking a seat, please?"

Amanda took a seat in one of the chairs, and Hank lifted up her bridal gown, revealing her garter strap. Hank brazenly removed the article with his teeth, which garnered a bevy of hoots and hollers from everyone in attendance.

"Ready, guys?" he asked, as he readied to slingshot the garter into a small army of single men who bought into the tradition.

The men were attempting to establish position, and Hank let the garter fly. It sailed into the air, and would find its way onto the table in front of a shy, yet dashing young man. Amanda looked over to where the garment landed, and saw Ashley's jaw drop. The man sported short brown hair and gray eyes. He was a little on the heavier set, but it appeared it didn't matter to Ashley. It was his eyes that attracted her. Ashley made her way over to his table and sat down beside him.

"Nice catch," she said.

"It wasn't really a catch," he said. "It just happened to land in front of me. You ending up the bridal bouquet, now that was a catch."

Ashley blushed. "Thank you," she said. "Although, I have to admit it was pure luck on my own part, as well."

"Given how you gave everyone the evil eye during the 'If anyone objects to these two' part of the ceremony," he said, "I think all of the ladies knew to give you your space."

Ashley laughed and extended her hand. "I'm Ashley Washburn."

The man took Ashley's hand and shook it. "Pleased to meet you," he said. "I'm Chuck MacDonald."

Ashley smiled. "Hello, Chuck," she said. "Did you come to the ceremony by yourself?"

Amanda and Hank looked on, and embraced each other.

"It looks like Ashley has found someone that has caught her eye," Amanda said.

"Kind of like how I caught your eye all those moons ago," Hank noted.

"Not necessarily in the exact same way," she said, "but sometimes that's all it takes; just one look, an appealing physical attribute, and that can start the ball rolling to something special."

"He looks a little on the heavy side to be swinging a redwood," Hank joked.

Amanda shot her husband a look. "I hate to break it to you, honey," she said, "but not all women go for a man's unit on first sight. It can be something simple like a nice pair of eyes, or a great smile."

Hank smiled. "I know that's what first attracted me to you," he stated. "I can get lost in your eyes for days."

Amanda blushed. "I felt the same way about yours when I first looked into them," she said. "Your cock was a bonus."

Hank winked at his wife. "You know," he said, "now that we're married, we should think about consummating things."

"Believe me," she said, "I am looking forward to it myself. But, we should wait until everyone's left the reception."

"I understand," he said; then, leaned in to whisper. "But, I can't wait to be inside of you again."

"I can't wait to have you inside me again, too," Amanda whispered back. "My loins are aching for you."

Hank sighed. "It's a shame we can't cut out early on everyone," he said, "so we can get started."

Amanda smiled. "Who says we can't?" she said.

Hank smiled back at Amanda, and took her hand in hers. He turned to the crowd, and made his announcement.

"May I have everyone's attention, please?" he said. "I would like to thank everyone for attending the ceremony today. Amanda and I are thankful for all of the support you have given us, and we have left each of you a little token of our appreciation."

Amanda added, "We have arranged to present small gift bags containing a memento commemorating our marriage today to everyone. We would like to present them to you personally, but Hank and I have some 'personal matters' to attend to. Again, thank you everyone for attending, and we hope all of you have a safe trip home."

The audience laughed over Amanda's 'personal matters' comment; then, applauded when the happy couple began to make their way from the tent. Hank and Amanda waved to everyone, as they passed; quickening their pace as they inched closer to the exit. The couple were about to make their way up the main house's porch steps when Ashley came rushing after them.

"Amanda," Ashley asked. "Are the two of you going upstairs to 'put Hank's nail in your coffin'?"

Amanda laughed. "I wouldn't use those words exactly," she said, "but if you mean 'do the nasty', then yes."

Ashley blinked. "You haven't told him yet?" she said.

"Told me about what?" Hank asked.

Amanda tried to play things nonchalantly. "What are you talking about, Ashley?" Amanda said.

"Don't play coy with me, chickie," Ashley said. "I saw the test when I used the bathroom during the reception."

Hank showed a look of concern. "Test, what test?" he asked. "Is there something wrong with Amanda?"

"Nothing's wrong, Hank." Ashley explained. "The test showed a positive result."

Amanda sighed. "Well, now that the cat's out of the bag," she reasoned, "it explains why I've been throwing up in the morning."

Hank stared at his wife. "Amanda," he asked. "Does this mean what I think it does?"

Amanda looked into Hank's eyes and told him the news. "I'll have to see the doctor to be certain," she said, "but if this is true, then yes, I'm pregnant."

Hank didn't say a word. He embraced his new wife, and kissed her softly. Amanda smiled at Hank; ready to start her new life as a spouse, and now, an expectant mother.

www.ingramcontent.com/pod-product-compliance
Lightning Source LLC
Chambersburg PA
CBHW072231170626
46813CB00003B/1170